SECRETS

OF THE

MAPLE CREEK

OTHER TITLES BY PATRICK C DUFFY

The Accidental Escort

SECRETS

OF THE

MAPLE CREEK

PATRICK C DUFFY

BIG MOOSE PUBLISHING

ISBN: 978-1-989840-82-5(sc)
ISBN: 978-1-989840-83-2(e)
Big Moose Publishing 02/25

For Trina

CONTENTS

Chapter 1 9
Chapter 2. 13
Chapter 3 23
Chapter 4 28
Chapter 5. 31
Chapter 6. 37
Chapter 7. 51
Chapter 8. 62
Chapter 9. 66
Chapter 10. 71
Chapter 11. 78
Chapter 12. 83
Chapter 13. 99
Chapter 14 114
Chapter 15. 124
Chapter 16. 132
Chapter 17. 146
Chapter 18. 152
Chapter 19. 162
Chapter 20. 175
Chapter 21. 181
Chapter 22. 190
Chapter 23. 198
Chapter 24. 212

Chapter 25 219
Chapter 26. 226
Chapter 27. 231
Chapter 28. 245
Chapter 29. 252
Chapter 30. 255
Chapter 31 266
Acknowledgments 271
About the Author 273

CHAPTER 1

The cell was cold. Not the kind of cold that chilled the skin, but the kind that crept deep into the bones, settling into the marrow like a slow, painful ache. Gavin Craite sat hunched in the corner, his back pressed against the damp stone wall, the heavy shackles on his wrists and ankles clinking faintly with every slight movement. His eyes, once sharp and full of fire, were now dulled with age and exhaustion. His hair, once black as a raven's wing, had grayed and thinned, and his face bore the deep lines of a man who had lived too long in the shadow of regret.

The cell was small, barely large enough for the iron cot in the corner and a bucket that reeked of stale waste. A single barred window near the ceiling let in a thin shaft of light, its weak glow falling across Gavin's tired face. He stared at the floor, not really seeing it, lost somewhere in the labyrinth of his own thoughts.

Now, he was here. Alone.

The clatter of the iron door at the end of the hallway echoed, pulling Gavin from his thoughts. He didn't look up, not at first. In the few hours he'd been here, Gavin had grown used to the sound of the footsteps in this place, the slow shuffle of guards and the distant whispers of other prisoners. But this time was different. The steps were softer, more deliberate.

A man approached the cell, dressed in black, the collar around his neck marking him as a priest. He stood outside the bars for a moment, holding a small leather-bound book in his hands, watching Gavin through the iron grate. Finally, the priest spoke, his voice soft but steady.

"Mr. Craite," the priest began, his tone gentle, "I'm Father Michael O'Connell. I've come to offer you absolution of your sins. Would you—"

"No," Gavin cut him off, his voice hoarse and low. He finally looked up, his tired eyes meeting Father O'Connell's. "I don't need your prayers. They won't do me no good."

The priest took a step closer. "It's never too late for redemption, my son. The Lord—"

"Don't call me that," Gavin growled, his voice edged with bitterness. He shifted slightly, the chains on his wrists clinking against the stone floor. "I ain't your son. And God ain't gonna forgive me for the things I've done. You waste your breath if you think he will."

The priest was silent for a moment, studying Gavin's weathered face, the deep lines etched by years of guilt and violence. "The Lord is merciful. Even the greatest sinner can find peace if he seeks it with a true heart."

Gavin let out a low, humorless laugh, shaking his head. "Ain't no mercy for a man like me. I've killed too many; ruined too many lives. Ain't no peace waiting for me on the other side."

Father O'Connell stood his ground. "There's always forgiveness, Mr. Craite. If you ask for it."

Gavin's eyes darkened, his voice quiet but firm. "I ain't asking for nothing."

The silence hung heavy between them, broken only by the distant sound of the wind rattling the bars of the window. Gavin leaned his head back against the wall, closing his eyes for a moment, as if trying to block out the weight of the priest's words. His mind wandered, drifting back to the memories he couldn't let go of and the memories that wouldn't let go of him.

When Gavin opened his eyes again, they were filled not with anger, but with something else. A kind of quiet desperation. He looked at the priest and spoke softly, almost pleading.

"If you want to help, give me some paper. And a pencil."

Father O'Connell blinked, taken aback by the request. "What for?"

"I need to write a letter," Gavin said, his voice raw.

"To my family."

Father O'Connell hesitated but nodded, understanding that this was perhaps the closest thing to redemption Gavin would allow himself. He turned and motioned to one of the guards, who brought over a small scrap of paper and a pencil. Gavin reached out with his shackled hands, taking them carefully, his rough fingers brushing against the fragile paper.

Father O'Connell stepped back, giving Gavin space, though he remained close enough to offer a final word.

"Perhaps," he said gently, "your letter could be a beginning. For peace."

Gavin didn't answer. He set the paper on his knee and stared at it for a long time, the pencil hovering just above it, shaking slightly in his hand. The words didn't come easy. They never had. But he knew he had to try, even if it was too late.

He wanted to explain, but he couldn't find the words. He stared at the empty page and thought back to when he was a boy…

CHAPTER 2

The sun hung low in the sky, casting a warm golden hue across the sprawling cattle farm. Dust kicked up around the hooves of the grazing bovine, and the distant sound of a horse's whinny echoed through the fields. A young Gavin Craite stood at the edge of the barn, his gaze drifting over the land he had known since as far back as he could remember. The place was both a sanctuary and a prison, a tapestry woven with memories—both joyous and heartbreaking.

Gavin and his older brother, Marek, had grown up in this vast expanse of rolling hills and open sky, bound together by their shared adventures and the burden of their family's struggles. As children, they would spend hours exploring the fields, imagining themselves as brave cowboys in a world full of danger and excitement. Those days were filled with laughter, the sound of their voices mingling with the calls of the cattle and the rustle of the wind through the tall grass.

One summer afternoon, they had ventured farther than usual, their curiosity pulling them toward the thick woods that bordered their land. "Let's see what's out there!" Marek had exclaimed, his eyes sparkling with mischief. Gavin had hesitated, feeling a gnawing worry at the pit of his stomach, but the thrill of adventure soon overpowered his fear.

"Come on Gavin, I'll take care of you if anything happens." Marek reassured him, noticing Gavin's apprehension.

As they forged deeper into the forest, they stumbled upon a clearing filled with wildflowers and the cheerful chirping of birds. It was a secret paradise, untouched and wild. They spent the day chasing each other through the blossoms, their laughter ringing through the trees as they rolled in the grass, the sun warming their backs.

As the day wore on, Gavin and Marek sprawled out in the soft grass, their chests heaving from exertion and laughter. The sweet scent of wildflowers mingled with the earthy aroma of the forest floor, creating a perfume that would forever remind them of this magical afternoon. Gavin plucked a daisy and twirled it between his fingers, watching as the petals blurred into a white pinwheel.

"Marek," he said, his voice filled with childish wonder, "d'you think we'll always be like this? Just us, exploring and having adventures?"

Marek propped himself up on one elbow, his hazel eyes twinkling with affection for his younger brother. "'Course we will, squirt. You're stuck with me forever, whether you like it or not."

Gavin's grin widened, and he playfully tossed the daisy at Marek's face. "Good," he chuckled.

As the afternoon sun began to dip lower in the sky, casting orange and pink across the land, the boys reluctantly decided it was time to head back home. They raced through the woods, ducking under low-hanging branches and leaping over fallen logs, their laughter echoing through the trees.

When they burst out of the bush and into the familiar expanse of their family's farm, they were greeted by the sight of their mother, Sharyn, hanging laundry on the clothesline. Her chestnut hair glowed in the fading sunlight, and her bright blue eyes crinkled with joy as she spotted her sons.

"There you are, my wildlings!" she called out, her voice warm with affection. Sharyn's eyes sparkled as she took in the sight of her sons, their clothes smudged with dirt and grass stains, hair tousled by the wind. "I was beginning to wonder if you'd decided to run off and join a band of outlaws!"

Gavin and Marek exchanged mischievous grins, their cheeks flushed from their forest adventure. They raced towards their mother, the scent of freshly laundered clothes mingling with the earthy aroma that clung to their skin.

"We found a secret meadow, Ma!" Gavin exclaimed, his blue eyes wide with excitement. "It was full of flowers and birds, and—"

"And a whole pack of coyotes that Gavin fought off single-handedly," Marek interrupted.

"Oh really? A whole pack you say?" Their mother entertained their imagination.

Sharyn enjoyed hearing the tall tales of Gavin and Marek's adventures, just as much as Gavin and Marek enjoyed telling them. They continued on with their story, playing off one another as they made their way inside the modest house to prepare for supper.

As the sun dipped below the horizon, painting the sky in vibrant orange and pink, the Craite family gathered around the weathered oak table for their evening meal. The aroma of freshly baked cornbread and hearty beef stew filled the small farmhouse kitchen, mingling with the scent of grass and meadow of the boys from their earlier adventures.

Sharyn set down a steaming pot in the center of the table, her eyes twinkling with warmth as she gazed at her family. "Alright, my wild ones," she said, a hint of playfulness in her voice, "time to fill those bellies after all your exploring."

Gavin and Marek eagerly took their seats, their faces still flushed from the day's excitement. Their father, Pat, joined them, his weathered hands rough from a long day's work in the fields. As Sharyn began ladling the rich, aromatic stew into their bowls, the family settled into a comfortable rhythm of conversation. The boys regaled their parents with tales of their forest adventure, their words tumbling over each other in their excitement. Pat listened with a bemused smile, his tired eyes softening as he watched his sons' animated faces.

"And then," Gavin exclaimed, gesturing wildly with his spoon, "we found this huge old tree with branches that reached up to the sky like—"

His words were suddenly cut short by a sharp, dry cough from Sharyn. The sound seemed to scrape against the warm atmosphere of the kitchen, causing a momentary pause in the conversation. Sharyn waved off their concerned looks with a forced smile.

"It's nothing, just a tickle in my throat," she assured them, her voice slightly hoarse. She took a sip of water, but the cough persisted, growing more intense with each passing moment. The boys exchanged worried glances as their mother's face reddened, her body shaking with the force of each ragged breath.

Pat's brow furrowed with concern as he watched his wife struggle. "Sharyn, love," he said, his voice low and tinged with worry, "that cough's been lingering for weeks now. Perhaps it's time we had the doctor take a look at you."

Sharyn tried to wave off his concern between coughs, but her attempts at reassurance were cut short by another bout of hacking. The sound echoed through the small kitchen, harsh and grating against the earlier warmth of their family dinner.

Gavin felt a knot of fear tighten in his stomach as he watched his mother, her face now pale and strained.

Sharyn's cough continued to worsen; her body wracked with each painful spasm. The boys watched in growing alarm as their mother's face turned an alarming shade of red, her eyes watering from the effort. Pat quickly stood and moved to her side, placing a comforting hand on her back.

"Easy now, love," he murmured, his voice tight with concern. "Just try to breathe slow and steady."

Gavin and Marek sat frozen; their earlier excitement forgotten as they watched their mother struggle for air. The rich aroma of the stew now seemed cloying and oppressive, mingling with the acrid scent of fear that permeated the room.

As Sharyn's coughing fit subsided, she sagged against Pat, her breath coming in ragged gasps. A fine sheen of sweat covered her brow, and her usual rosy cheeks were as pale as snow. She excused herself from the table and made her way upstairs to their bedroom, leaving the table deathly silent. Pat, Gavin and Marek finished their suppers without saying another word to one another, then cleaned up as best they could.

Gavin and Marek fell asleep that night and many nights after, in their beds listening to their mother suffering from coughing fits so bad she'd often have trouble catching her breath.

Days later, their father left them to care for the

farm as he and their mother made trail for town to see the doctor.

"I'm sure the doc will fix mom up" Marek tried to reassure Gavin.

But, as it was in those times, the carefree days of childhood were often shadowed by the harsh realities of life on the farm. Their mother's illness had loomed over them like a dark cloud, her health deteriorating with each passing season. Gavin remembered the sound of her cough echoing through the wooden halls of their home, a sound that made their father's stern demeanor even harder to bear.

"Boys, keep the cattle in line," their father would bark, his voice like a whip cracking through the air. He was becoming a hard man as he watched his wife deteriorate, frustrated with his inability to help her, his life etched in lines of toil and sorrow. He now had little patience for childhood antics, believing every moment should be spent working. "There's no time for playing when there's work to be done."

But in the quiet moments, when their father was busy with chores, Gavin and Marek found solace in each other's company. They would sit beneath the old oak tree near the barn, sharing dreams of the future while the world around them faded away. "One day, this'll be our ranch," Marek would say, his eyes full of determination. "We'll have cattle that graze for miles and a house big enough for our families."

Gavin had smiled, feeling the warmth of hope

wash over him, but even then, he sensed the heaviness of reality peering just beyond the horizon. Their mother's health continued to decline, and their father fell deeper and deeper into despair, much the same with the state of their farm.

Gavin and Marek would do their best to complete their chores to appease their ever-deteriorating father and then they would venture off past the fields and into the valley to escape the increasingly darkening cloud cast over their homelife. It was during this time of worry that Gavin and Marek faced their most terrifying adventure—a brush with a cougar that would leave Gavin with a scar that would forever mark his cheek. They had been out herding cattle when they noticed one of the calves straying too close to the forest's edge.

"Gavin, we have to get it back!" Marek shouted, and without thinking, they raced after the calf, hearts pounding with adrenaline.

They were almost upon it when they caught sight of a thick tail flashing above the brush and then erupting in chaos. The cougar burst into the clearing, its massive frame blocking their path. Gavin's heart raced as he instinctively stepped back, but the calf had nowhere to go. In a heartbeat, the ferocious cat pounced at the calf, sending it sprawling to the ground.

Gavin's protective instincts kicked in. "Get behind me!" he yelled to Marek as he lunged forward, adrenaline coursing through him. But the cougar was faster. It turned its ferocious gaze on Gavin, and in that moment, time seemed to freeze.

With a menacing growl, the muscular feline charged. Gavin barely had time to react. He felt a sharp pain as the creature's claw raked across his face, leaving a deep gash that would scar him for life.

Marek screamed, a sound filled with terror, but it broke through Gavin's haze, grabbing a heavy stick, he swung at the predator, striking it firmly on it's front leg joint. The strike appeared to cause enough pain or surprise at the cougar briefly retreated from its attack.

"Run!" he managed to shout, stumbling backward as the cougar minced in discomfort. Marek didn't hesitate, darting away with all his might. Gavin followed suit, the adrenaline pushing them forward as they raced back toward the safety of the barn.

The sleek, muscular cougar did not give chase to its prey. Instead, it stood proudly over the fallen calf, its eyes gleaming with satisfaction and its fur glistening in the sunlight. The young calf had met its demise at the hands of this powerful predator, who had emerged victorious from the hunt. The cougar's sharp claws and teeth had left deep marks on the calf's body, a striking contrast against its soft fur. The air was thick with the smell of blood and sweat, a reminder of the wildness and ferocity of nature. As the gigantic cat dragged its prize into the bush, the surrounding forest fell silent in reverence for this skilled hunter.

Arriving home, out of breath and Gavin with

significant cuts to the left side of his face, their mother was able to, for the moment, overcome her illness to care for her injured son. She cleaned and dressed the wound as best she could and held her son until he fell asleep.

They seldom spoke of the encounter afterward, the fear and pain buried beneath layers of their shared experiences. But the scar on Gavin's cheek became a silent reminder of that day—of their childhood's fleeting innocence and the harsh realities that followed.

CHAPTER 3

The days grew shorter and colder as autumn settled over the farm, painting the landscape amber and gold. But the beauty of the season was lost on the Craite family, as Sharyn's condition continued to deteriorate. Her once-vibrant laughter had faded to a weak, raspy chuckle, often interrupted by fits of violent coughing that left her gasping for air.

Gavin and Marek watched helplessly as their mother withered away before their eyes. Her chestnut hair, once so radiant in the sunlight, now hung limp and dull around her gaunt face. Her bright blue eyes, which had always crinkled with warmth when she smiled, now seemed sunken and glazed with fever. The boys would take turns sitting by her bedside, holding her frail hand and pretending not to notice the flecks of blood that stained her handkerchief after each coughing fit.

As winter approached, Sharyn's condition worsened rapidly. The coughing fits became more frequent and violent, wracking her frail body with such force that it seemed she might shatter. The boys would wake in the night to the sound of her struggles, muffled sobs from their father's room, and the acrid smell of sickness that permeated the house.

One particularly brutal night, Gavin crept from his bed, unable to bear the sound of his mother's suffering. He found her propped up on pillows, her face ashen in the dim lamplight. Her chest heaved with each labored breath, as beads of sweat gathered on her forehead.

"Ma," Gavin whispered, his voice cracking with emotion. "Can I get you anything?"

Sharyn's eyes fluttered open, focusing on Gavin with effort. A weak smile tugged at her lips. "My sweet boy," she rasped, reaching out a trembling hand. "Just sit with me a while."

Gavin took her hand, alarmed at how cold and fragile it felt in his grasp. He perched on the edge of the bed, trying to ignore the sour smell of illness that clung to the sheets. In the flickering lamplight, he could see the blue veins standing out starkly against his mother's pale skin.

"Tell me a story," Sharyn whispered, her voice barely audible. "About your adventures with Marek."

Gavin swallowed hard, fighting back tears. He began to speak, his voice low and soothing, recounting their escapades in the meadow, embellishing the tales with fantastic creatures and daring feats. As he spoke, he watched his mother's face relax, a shadow of her old smile playing across her lips.

But midway through a tale of battling imaginary dragons, Sharyn's body was seized by another violent coughing fit. Gavin held her hand tightly as she shook, her breath coming in ragged gasps. When the fit subsided, she slumped back against the pillows, utterly spent.

"Ma?" Gavin whispered, fear clutching at his heart.

Sharyn's eyes fluttered open, clouded with pain and fatigue. "I'm here, love," she murmured. "Just... just tired."

The door creaked open, and Pat entered, his face haggard with worry and lack of sleep. He nodded to Gavin, placing a gentle hand on his shoulder. "Go on now, son. Let your mother rest."

Gavin nodded silently and slipped out of the room; his heart heavy. As he closed the door behind him, he caught a glimpse of his father gently wiping Sharyn's brow with a damp cloth, murmuring soft words of comfort.

The days that followed blurred together in a haze of worry and exhaustion. Sharyn's condition continued to deteriorate, her once melodious voice reduced to a feeble whisper. The boys took turns sitting with her, reading her favorite books or simply holding her hand as she drifted in and out of consciousness.

One crisp autumn morning, as the first rays of sunlight filtered through the curtains, Gavin awoke to an eerie silence. The usual sounds of his mother's labored breathing were absent, replaced by a stillness that sent a chill down his spine. He crept to his parents' room, his heart pounding in his chest. As he pushed open the door, he saw his father slumped in the chair beside the bed, his face buried in his hands. Marek was already there, standing frozen at the foot of the bed, his eyes wide with disbelief.

Gavin's gaze fell upon his mother's still form. Marek placed an arm around his brother. Sharyn lay motionless, her face peaceful for the first time in months. The room was thick with the scent of illness and wilting flowers, the air heavy with unspoken grief.

"Ma?" Gavin whispered; his voice barely audible. He took a hesitant step forward, hoping against hope that she was just sleeping deeply. But as he drew closer, he could see the unnatural stillness of her chest, the waxy pallor of her skin.

Pat looked up, his eyes red-rimmed and hollow. "She's gone, boys."

The following days were filled with sorrow and darkness. The laughter that once echoed through the fields grew quieter. Their father's grief turned to bitterness, and the weight of the farm became heavier with every passing season. Gavin and Marek relied on each other more than ever, their bond forged in the fires of hardship and shared memories. They learned to find joy in the little things—watching the sunrise over the fields, the taste of fresh bread baked by their mother before her illness, and the nights spent under a blanket of stars. Sharyn had been a shelter for the boys. Without her, there was no cover for them. Pat was unable to provide the love and support the boys, especially Gavin, needed. In turn they grew increasingly frustrated with one another, often resulting in the boys fleeing their home for the sanctuary of the fields to escape their father's increasingly violent behavior, a result of grief and cheap whiskey.

The shadows of loss were never far behind, and Gavin often found himself haunted by the memories of their mother, her soft voice whispering lullabies in the dark, and their father's stern gaze, hardened by grief. Life on the farm had shaped them, leaving indelible marks on their hearts and souls. As Gavin stood there, looking out over the land, he knew that those memories would always be a part of him—both a blessing and a curse.

CHAPTER 4

The years that followed Sharyn's passing were marked by a slow, inexorable decline. Pat Craite, once a pillar of strength and determination, crumbled under the strain of his grief. The bottle became his constant companion, cheap whiskey burning away the pain of loss and drowning the memories of happier times. The acrid smell of alcohol clung to him like a second skin, mingling with the musty odor of unwashed clothes and neglect.

At first, his descent into alcoholism was gradual. A nip here and there to take the edge off, a glass or two in the evening to help him sleep. But soon, the amber liquid became a necessity, as vital to him as the air he breathed. The farm, once a thriving testament to the Craite family's hard work, began to wither under his negligent gaze.

Fields that had once burst with golden wheat now lay fallow, choked with weeds and thistles. The barn's red paint peeled away in great flakes, revealing weathered gray wood beneath. The fences sagged, allowing cattle to wander freely across the overgrown pastures. The farmhouse itself, once a warm and welcoming haven, fell into disrepair. Shutters hung askew, the porch steps creaked ominously, and the roof leaked during every rainstorm.

Pat's temper, always quick to flare, became a raging inferno fueled by alcohol and grief. His words, once merely stern, turned cruel and cutting. The sound of breaking glass and angry shouts became a nightly occurrence, echoing through the dilapidated halls of their once-happy home.

Gavin and Marek, now on the cusp of manhood, bore the brunt of their father's anger.

As their father's descent into alcoholism deepened, Marek stepped forward to fill the void. At just eighteen, he shouldered the responsibility of the farm and family, his lean frame hardening with muscle as he took on the backbreaking work. His hazel eyes, once bright with boyish mischief, now held a determined glint as he rose before dawn each day to tend to the livestock and fields.

Gavin watched in awe as his older brother transformed, becoming the pillar of strength, their father had once been. Marek's hands, once soft from childhood play, grew calloused and weathered. The sun bronzed his skin, and his light brown hair bleached to a golden hue under its relentless rays.

With unwavering dedication, Marek breathed new life into the neglected farm. He mended fences, his strong arms swinging the hammer with practiced ease. The rhythmic pounding echoed across the fields, a steady heartbeat bringing the land back from the brink. He rose before dawn each day, the cool morning air biting at his skin as he made his way to the barn. The musty scent of hay and leather filled his nostrils as he set about his chores, milking the cows and feeding the chickens.

Gavin, now sixteen, worked alongside his brother, his lean muscles aching from the unaccustomed labor. Together, they toiled under the scorching sun, sweat beading on their brows as they plowed the fields and planted crops. The rich scent of freshly turned earth surrounded them, mingling with the tang of their own perspiration.

CHAPTER 5

"Are you heading out to the dance tonight?" Gavin asked Marek.

"Nah, what's the point? There's lots to get done 'round here, I don't wanna waste the time it'll take to ride into town and back. I could be using that to tend to things here."

Gavin looked over at their father, who was passed out in his chair snoring away. "Yeah, I can see why you'd wanna stick around here. And who knows, maybe dad'll pull himself together and you two can go for a walk and clear the air."

Marek thought about it for a while longer.

"And who knows, maybe if you left for town for a reason other than picking up supplies and feed, you'd find someone to spend your time with other than me." Gavin added.

"You know, now that you mention it, it would be nice not having to listen to you for a while." Marek responded.

Their laughter echoed through the small cabin before they emerged into the warm spring air. They made their way to the dugout, a natural pool surrounded by tall trees and wildflowers. The crystal-clear water beckoned them in for a refreshing dip, washing away any traces of dirt and sweat from their morning chores. After drying off and dressing in their finest yet humble attire, they mounted their horses and set off towards town. The vibrant greens of the countryside were dotted with colorful flowers, a testament to the new season. As they rode, birds sang overhead and the sun shone down on them, making everything feel alive and full of possibilities. Their destination was the spring social, an event known for bringing together the entire community in celebration of the changing seasons. With excitement and anticipation building, they urged their horses to go faster, eager to join in on the festivities ahead.

When they arrived, they tied their horses to a post and made their way to the social where there was food and drinks, and the hall was buzzing with the sound of laughter, fiddles, and boots scuffling across the floor. Gavin and Marek stood near the entrance, their backs pressed against the rough wooden wall, a half-empty cup of whiskey dangling from his fingers. Gavin had come for a distraction, maybe to forget the long, hard days of labor that marked every week, watching his father drink himself to sleep each night.

Through the sea of dancing bodies, he saw her. Time seemed to slow. The music faded to a dull hum, and the sounds of the crowded hall slipped away, leaving only – her. She stood near the edge of the dance floor, laughing with her friends, the soft candlelight illuminating her long, dark hair. Gavin's breath caught in his chest. He had never seen anyone like her before. She was tall and graceful, her face radiant with warmth. Her smile was enough to brighten the dimly lit room, but it was the little freckles across her nose that struck him—small, delicate dots that made her beauty seem all the more real. She looked like she belonged in another world, one far kinder than the rough one Gavin knew.

Without thinking, he raised the bottle to his lips, the burn of the whiskey giving him a bit of courage. His heart pounded in his chest as he pushed himself off the wall and made his way through the crowd. Normally, he might have hesitated, but the alcohol made him bold. His eyes stayed locked on her, and for the first time in his life, he could see his future as clear as day.

When he finally reached her, she looked at him, her shy gaze meeting his. She smiled, and in that moment, it was as if the whole room disappeared.

"May I have this dance?" Gavin's voice was rough, unpolished, but there was something genuine in the way he asked, something that made her cheeks flush a soft pink.

She hesitated for just a moment, then nodded, placing her hand gently in his. "I'd like that."

As they stepped onto the dance floor, the music seemed to envelop them, wrapping them in its lively beat. At first, their movements were awkward and hesitant—Gavin was not known for his dancing skills, and the girl's shyness only added to their stumbling steps. But as they continued to sway and twirl, something shifted between them. They found a natural rhythm, moving together as if they had been dancing together for years.

Gavin couldn't tear his eyes away from her. Every time she looked up at him, he felt a fluttering in his chest, a sensation he couldn't quite put into words but knew was special. The girl, too, was beginning to let go of her shyness, a soft smile gracing her lips as she moved with Gavin. She had noticed him the moment he walked in, drawn to his confident presence and kind eyes. As they danced, the world around them faded away until it felt like there were only the two of them on the dance floor, lost in the music and the magic of the moment.

As the dance ended, neither of them wanted to let go. Gavin gently took her hand and led her outside, away from the noise of the hall. The cool night air wrapped around them as they stepped into the quiet street, the stars twinkling overhead.

"I'm Gavin," he said, breaking the silence, his voice a little softer now.

"Hi Gavin. I'm Shannon," she replied, her gaze flicking between him and the ground as if she couldn't quite believe they were out here together.

They stood for a moment, just looking at each other. Gavin didn't know what came over him, but before he could stop himself, he leaned in, brushing a soft kiss against her lips. It was gentle, almost hesitant, but the electricity between them was undeniable.

Shannon blinked, her heart racing, but she didn't pull away. Instead, she smiled, her hand finding his.

Gavin and Shannon slipped away from the dance, finding a secluded spot nearby where they could indulge in their passion for each other. For Gavin, it was his first time being embraced by a woman - reveling in her soft features, plush lips, and the sensation of her tongue against his. They lost themselves in each other's embrace for hours, though to them it felt like only moments.

Much later, Marek discovered Gavin still entranced with his new love. Awkwardly and after several efforts, Marek was able to interrupt them from their passioned fueled trance long enough to let them know that Shannon's friends were worried and looking for her. Reluctantly, Shannon and Gavin made their way back to the dance, accompanied by Marek who followed a step behind. Upon arriving at the dance and seeing Shannon's friends running over to her, Gavin made a desperate attempt to secure another moment with her.

"When can I see you again?" Gavin asked with desperation.

"You can see me any time you'd like, come find me at my family's farm. We're the McAllister's, just south of the Maple Creek, before the Sutherland's farm.

"I can find that." Gavin said with confidence.

Gavin couldn't contain his growing grin as he rode back to the farm, the name "Shannon McAllister" rolling off his tongue with a sense of wonder. Every thought was consumed with her beauty, from the way her hair shone in the moonlight to the delicate scent that lingered on his skin after their kiss. He could still feel the softness of her lips against his own and the electricity that sparked between them. He eagerly recounted every moment over and over to Marek who was growing more and more tired every time he started, though Gavin did not notice. He was lost in the memory of this new passion.

"What about you? Gavin asked. "Did you find a young lady to pass your time with?"

Marek, having had a few whiskeys by this point and letting his guard down, "Gavin, I don't feel the same way about women as you apparently do."

Gavin didn't appear to notice the meaning of Marek's words, as he was still living in the memory of this magical evening. Although Marek knew Gavin hadn't processed what he had said, he was relieved to have been able to say it out loud.

CHAPTER 6

The sun had barely crested the horizon when Gavin set out for the McAllister farm, his heart pounding with anticipation. He had spent hours the night before preparing, polishing his boots until they gleamed, and pressing his best shirt until every wrinkle surrendered. Now, as he rode across the dewy fields, the crisp morning air nipped at his cheeks, but he hardly noticed, his mind consumed with thoughts of Shannon.

As he approached the McAllister property, the landscape transformed. Unlike the Craite's weathered farm, the McAllister land was a picture of prosperity. Neat fences lined well-tended fields where fat cattle grazed contentedly. The barn, freshly painted a deep red, stood proudly against the backdrop of rolling hills. The farmhouse itself was a stately two-story structure, its white clapboard siding gleaming in the morning light.

Gavin's stomach churned with a mixture of excitement and nervousness as he approached the McAllister farmhouse. The scent of freshly baked bread wafted through the air, mingling with the sweet fragrance of blooming flowers that lined the well-maintained path to the front door. He took a deep breath, straightened his collar, and knocked.

The door swung open, revealing Mr. McAllister, a tall, broad-shouldered man with a stern expression etched onto his weathered face. His piercing gaze seemed to look right through Gavin, assessing every detail of his appearance and demeanor.

"Can I help you, young man?" Mr. McAllister's voice was gruff, tinged with suspicion.

Gavin swallowed hard, willing his voice not to waver. "Good morning, sir. I'm Gavin Craite. I've come to call on Shannon, if she's available."

Mr. McAllister's eyes narrowed slightly, his gaze boring into Gavin with an intensity that made the young man want to shrink back. For a moment, silence hung heavy between them, broken only by the distant lowing of cattle and the rustle of leaves in the gentle breeze.

"Craite, you say?" Mr. McAllister's voice was measured, betraying neither approval nor disdain. "Pat Craite's boy?"

Gavin nodded, fighting the urge to look away. "Yes, sir. That's right."

Mr. McAllister seemed to consider this for a moment, his weathered hand stroking his chin thoughtfully. Finally, he stepped aside, gesturing for Gavin to enter. "Come in, then. Shannon's just finished helping her mother with the morning chores."

Gavin stepped into the McAllister home, immediately struck by the warmth and comfort that seemed to radiate from every corner. The entryway opened into a spacious living room, where a fire crackled merrily in the hearth despite the mild spring weather. The rich scent of wood smoke mingled with the aroma of fresh-baked bread and something sweet—perhaps apple pie—creating an inviting atmosphere that was a stark contrast to the neglected Craite farmhouse.

As his eyes adjusted to the interior light, Gavin noticed the details that spoke of a home well-loved and cared for. Handmade quilts draped over well-worn armchairs, their intricate patterns telling stories of generations past. Family portraits adorned the walls, capturing moments of joy and milestones celebrated. The polished wood floors creaked softly underfoot, bearing witness to years of footsteps and laughter.

From the kitchen, Gavin heard the clatter of dishes and the soft murmur of voices. His heart leapt as he recognized Shannon's melodious laugh among them. Mr. McAllister led him towards the sound, and as they entered the bright, airy kitchen, Gavin's breath caught in his throat.

There she was, even more beautiful than he

remembered. Shannon stood by the sink, her hands covered in soap suds as she washed dishes. Her fiery red curls were pulled back into a loose braid, with a few wayward strands framing her delicate features. The morning sunlight streaming through the window caught the copper highlights in her hair, creating a halo effect that took Gavin's breath away. She wore a simple cotton dress, its pale blue fabric complementing her fair skin and bringing out the vibrant green of her eyes.

As Shannon turned and caught sight of Gavin, her face lit up with a radiant smile that made his heart skip a beat. She quickly dried her hands on her apron and moved towards him, her eyes sparkling with joy and a hint of shyness.

"Gavin," she said softly, her voice like music to his ears. "You came."

Before Gavin could respond, Mrs. McAllister emerged from the pantry, her arms laden with jars of preserves. She was a plump, motherly woman with Shannon's same vibrant black hair, though hers was streaked with silver. Her warm brown eyes crinkled at the corners as she smiled at Gavin.

"Well now, who's this handsome young man?" she asked, setting down her burden and wiping her hands on her apron.

Shannon's cheeks flushed a pretty pink as she made the introductions. "Ma, Pa, this is Gavin Craite. Gavin, these are my parents, Thomas and Margaret

McAllister."

Gavin nodded respectfully to each of them, acutely aware of Mr. McAllister's scrutinizing gaze. "It's a pleasure to meet you both," he said, his voice steady despite the nervous flutter in his stomach.

Mrs. McAllister's warm smile put him slightly at ease. "Well, you've come at a good time, Gavin. We were just about to have some fresh-baked scones with our morning tea. Why don't you join us?"

Before Gavin could respond, the back door burst open and two young boys tumbled in, their clothes smudged with dirt and their faces flushed from play. They skidded to a halt when they saw Gavin, their eyes wide with curiosity.

Shannon laughed, the sound like bells in the suddenly quiet kitchen. "And these are my little brothers, Liam and Aiden," she introduced.

The two boys eyed Gavin with a mixture of curiosity and suspicion. Aiden, the older of the two at about twelve years old, stepped forward boldly. "Are you Shannon's beau?" he asked, his freckled face scrunched up in scrutiny.

Liam, no more than nine, piped up from behind his brother. "Yeah, are you gonna marry her?"

Shannon's face flushed an even deeper shade of pink as she swatted playfully at her brothers. "Hush, you two! Don't be rude to our guest."

Mrs. McAllister chuckled warmly. "Boys, why don't you go wash up for tea? And mind you scrub those hands properly this time."

As the boys scampered off, their laughter echoing through the house, Mr. McAllister cleared his throat. "Well then, shall we move to the parlor for tea?"

The family, with Gavin in tow, settled into the cozy parlor. Sunlight streamed through lace curtains, casting dappled patterns on the polished hardwood floor. The room was filled with the comforting scent of beeswax and lavender, mingling with the aroma of freshly baked scones. Gavin perched on the edge of an overstuffed armchair, acutely aware of his rough hands and work-worn clothes in this refined setting.

Mrs. McAllister bustled about, setting out delicate China teacups and a steaming pot of tea. The scones, golden-brown and still warm from the oven, were arranged on a silver platter alongside small jars of homemade jam and clotted cream. The aroma of the freshly baked goods filled the room, making Gavin's mouth water.

As they settled in, Mr. McAllister fixed Gavin with a steady gaze. "So, young man, tell us about yourself. What are your plans for the future?"

Gavin swallowed hard; his throat suddenly dry. He reached for his teacup, the delicate material feeling fragile in his calloused hands. "Well, sir, I've been working our family farm with my brother Marek. We've been trying to get it back to what it once was."

Shannon's eyes softened as she looked at Gavin, a small smile playing on her lips. She could sense his nervousness and wanted to put him at ease. "Gavin's been working so hard," she added, her voice warm with admiration. "He and his brother have really turned things around on their farm."

Mr. McAllister nodded slowly; his expression unreadable. "And what of your schooling? Do you have plans beyond the farm?"

Gavin felt a flush creep up his neck. "I... I haven't had much schooling, sir. But I've been reading when I can, trying to learn more about modern farming techniques."

Mrs. McAllister, sensing the tension, quickly interjected. "That's wonderful, dear. There's no substitute for hard work and a willingness to learn." She passed around the plate of scones, the buttery aroma filling the room. The pleasant smell did little to ease the tension, though, as Mr. McAllister fixed Gavin with a piercing gaze.

"Reading is admirable," Mr. McAllister said, his tone neutral but pointed. "But farming is unpredictable. Seasons change, and fortunes rise and fall with them. How do you plan to provide stability for a family, young man?"

Gavin met his gaze, his hands gripping his knees to steady himself. "I understand your concern, sir. It's true, farming can be uncertain, but my brother and I have worked hard to build something lasting. We've got good soil, strong cattle, and plans to expand. I'm not afraid of hard work, and I'll do whatever it takes to provide for Shannon…or I mean, you know." Gavin was clearly flustered.

The room seemed to hold its breath. Shannon, seated beside her mother, gave Gavin an encouraging nod, her fingers lightly brushing his as if to lend him strength.

Mr. McAllister leaned back in his chair, folding his arms. "Hard work is important, no doubt. But a man's character and resolve are tested in ways beyond the fields. Tell me, Gavin, what do you believe makes a man?"

The question caught Gavin off guard, but he didn't falter. He straightened in his seat, his voice steady. "A man is someone who respects others and commands respect from others, sir. Someone who listens, stands by the ones they love, and protects them, no matter what. He's someone who shares the family burdens and their joys and does everything he can to make those he loves and cares for happy."

Mrs. McAllister smiled softly, her eyes darting toward Shannon, who was now beaming with pride. One of Shannon's brothers, seated nearby, raised an eyebrow but said nothing, clearly curious about Gavin's response.

"And you think you can be that man?" Mr. McAllister pressed, his tone almost challenging.

"Yes, sir," Gavin replied without hesitation. "I know I can."

For a moment, there was only the crackle of the

fire in the hearth, the weight of Mr. McAllister's scrutiny bearing down on Gavin. Finally, he let out a long breath and unfolded his arms.

"Well," he said gruffly, "time will tell, I suppose."

"Father," Shannon interjected, her tone both firm and pleading. "Gavin's a good man. I care for him. Isn't that what matters most?"

Mr. McAllister's eyes softened slightly as he looked at his daughter. "What matters, Shannon, is that you have a secure and happy life. If this young man can provide that…" He paused, glancing at Gavin. "Then he'll have my blessing. But I'll be watching, son. Don't think for a second that I won't."

Gavin nodded, understanding the seriousness of the promise he was making. "I wouldn't expect anything less, sir."

Just then, Mrs. McAllister stood, smoothing her apron. "Well, that's enough serious talk for one evening. Dinner is ready, and I won't have my roast going cold."

The tension eased as the family rose and made their way to the dining room. Shannon stayed back a moment, her hand slipping into Gavin's.

"You handled that well," she whispered, her eyes filled with affection.

Gavin smiled, the warmth of her touch calming his nerves. "I'd do anything for you, Shannon."

"And I'd do the same for you," she replied softly before leading him into the dining room, where the rest of the family awaited.

The dining room, bathed in the warm glow of a chandelier, was filled with the clinking of cutlery and the soft murmurs of conversation. The roast sat in the center of the table, accompanied by steaming bowls of potatoes, carrots, and a loaf of crusty bread. Despite the inviting spread, the atmosphere felt tense, the gravity of Mr. McAllister's earlier scrutiny lingering over the meal.

"So, Gavin," Mr. McAllister began, cutting into his roast with a deliberate air, "what are your long-term plans for the farm? Expansion? Diversification? Or will you simply rely on good weather and luck?"

Gavin swallowed his bite of potato, taking a moment to gather his thoughts. "We're working on expanding, sir. My brother and I have been clearing more land, and we're considering breeding a sturdier line of cattle. We've also been experimenting with crop rotation to keep the soil healthy."

"Experimenting, are you?" Mr. McAllister's tone held a trace of skepticism. "Farming isn't the place for guesswork. It's a business. One wrong move, and you could lose everything."

"Father," Shannon interjected, her voice firm but respectful. "Gavin knows what he's doing. He and Marek have already turned that farm around, and they're doing better than most in the area."

Mr. McAllister's gaze shifted to his daughter; his fork paused mid-air. "Better isn't always enough,

Shannon. A marriage needs stability. Security."

"Really, father, we've only just met. I think you're being overly protective and unreasonable," Shannon said, her tone unwavering. "I grew up on a farm, remember? I know what it takes, and I'm not afraid of the work or the risks. Gavin has already proven he's capable, and more importantly, he makes me happy."

Mr. McAllister took a deep breath and looked at his daughter in the eye. "Perhaps if I had taken more of an interest in your suitors, we could've avoided the unpleasantness of Mr. Ellis Grady."

Shannon lowered her eyes, "Yes, well Ellis was much less the man than Gavin has already proven to be. And Ellis and I only spent time together a few times before I told him not to come around any more." She defended herself.

"I would've ensured he hadn't ever come around." Mr. McAllister interjected.

"Father. This is hardly polite conversation, especially considering this is Gavin's first visit to our home." Shannon pleaded.

Mrs. McAllister, seated at the other end of the table, gave a small nod of approval, her eyes twinkling as she glanced at Gavin. "Happiness is worth more than gold, I always say," she chimed in. "You two seem well-suited to each other."

Shannon's brothers exchanged glances, one of them offering a faint smirk as if amused by the tension. "So, Gavin," the younger of the two said, breaking the momentary silence, "do you hunt? Father likes a good hunting story."

"I've done a bit of hunting," Gavin replied. "Mostly for necessity, not sport. My brother and I had a run-in with a cougar once. That was an experience I wouldn't want to repeat."

Shannon's eyes widened. "You never told me about that!"

"It's not exactly a tale for the dinner table," Gavin said with a sheepish smile, trying to lighten the mood.

Mrs. McAllister laughed softly, her hands folding in her lap. "Oh, I like him, Shannon. He's charming, even under pressure."

Mr. McAllister's expression remained stern, though he said nothing, focusing instead on his plate.

As the meal progressed, the tension began to ease. Shannon's brothers asked Gavin more questions, this time about the farm and his plans, and even shared a few of their own stories. Mrs. McAllister's warmth filled the room, her light humor and kind words helping to soften the edges of the conversation.

But Mr. McAllister's silence loomed, and every so often, his disapproving gaze would settle on Gavin.

When dessert was served—apple pie with fresh cream—Shannon leaned close to Gavin, her voice low. "You're doing great," she whispered.

Gavin offered a small, grateful smile, though the fervor of Mr. McAllister's judgment still hung heavily on his shoulders.

After the meal, as the family moved to the sitting room for tea, Gavin caught Mr. McAllister's eye. Despite the warmth of the others, the patriarch's approval remained elusive.

Later, as Gavin helped Shannon clear the table, he leaned in close. "I wish your father liked me," he murmured, his voice barely audible. Shannon paused, her hand brushing his. "You don't need his approval, Gavin. You just need mine." She teased.

Gavin met her gaze, his resolve firming. He would do everything in his power to earn Mr. McAllister's respect—not for his own sake, but for Shannon's. Whatever it took. The rest of the evening overcame the initial awkwardness and carried on as pleasantly as possible, thanks in large part to Mrs. McAllister keeping Mr. McAllister occupied with chores. Gavin said his farewells, and Shannon escorted him to his horse. "I'm glad you came calling, don't worry about father, he's just a little over protective. I had a less-than-ideal experience with a previous suitor who felt he could lay his hands on me as he suited. I had to fend him off, until my father heard me pleading for help. He came over and… well, let's just say he made sure Ellis learned a lesson in how to treat women."

"I would never hurt you, Shannon." Gavin promised.

"Good." Shannon said before looking around to ensure nobody was watching, then leaned in and gave Gavin a kiss with such passion he nearly fell backwards.

The moment was interrupted by Liam and Aiden giggling in the bushes behind them. "I'm telling Pa," they teased.

"I guess I better go, then" Gavin said as he mounted his horse. "I'll call again."

"You better." Shannon replied, sliding her hand down his leg as his horse took off.

CHAPTER 7

Weeks had passed since Gavin first visited the McAllister farm. He and Shannon spent as much time together as they could. One morning, the early summer sun hung high in the sky, casting a warm glow over Gavin's cattle farm. The air was thick with the sweet scent of blooming wildflowers and the gentle sounds of nature. It was a perfect day, one that seemed to promise magic, and Gavin felt it in every fiber of his being as he and Shannon made their way toward the secluded creek that wound through his family's land.

"Where are you taking me?" Shannon asked playfully, her laughter dancing on the breeze as Gavin led her by the hand.

"To our secret spot," he replied with a grin, excitement bubbling within him. He had discovered the creek as a child, a hidden treasure nestled beneath the towering trees, and now it felt like the perfect place to share something special with Shannon.

When they reached the clearing, Shannon's eyes widened in awe. The creek glistened in the sunlight, its water sparkling like diamonds as it flowed gently over smooth stones. Wild flowers lined the bank, and the soft rustle of leaves created a soothing symphony.

"It's beautiful," she breathed, stepping closer to the water's edge, her long hair catching the light in a halo around her face. Gavin watched her, captivated by the way she seemed to glow in the sunlight, her smile radiant and infectious.

"I wanted to show you this place because it's special to me," he said, stepping closer. "I've dreamed of sharing it with someone I love."

Shannon turned to him, her gaze searching his face. "And you love me?"

Gavin took a deep breath, the gravity of the moment settling over him. "With all my heart, Shannon. I never thought I could feel this way about anyone until I met you."

Her eyes sparkled with emotion as she stepped into his embrace. Time seemed to stand still as they held each other, the world around them fading into a blur. Gavin's heart raced, a warmth spreading through him that he had never known before.

"I love you too, Gavin," she whispered, pressing against his chest, her voice soft yet filled with conviction. "I can't imagine my life without you, now."

As if drawn together by an unseen force, they leaned into each other, their lips meeting in a kiss that felt like a promise—a vow of love and devotion. Gavin's hands tangled in her hair as he deepened the kiss, his heart swelling with joy.

They spent the afternoon by the creek, talking about their dreams and future together, their laughter mingling with the sound of the water. Gavin told her of his plans for the farm, how he wanted to expand it, to have a family of their own one day. Shannon listened intently, her eyes sparkling with excitement.

"I want a home filled with love," she said, her voice soft. "A place where our children can grow up, just like you did."

Gavin's heart raced at the thought of a future with her. "I want that too, Shannon. I can see us raising a family here, surrounded by the beauty of this land."

As the sun began to dip low in the sky, casting a golden glow over the creek, the air was charged with a palpable energy. Gavin felt an overwhelming urge to express his love in the most intimate way. He took Shannon's hand, leading her further into the shade of the trees, where the world felt both safe and secluded.

They found a soft patch of grass beneath an ancient oak tree, and Gavin spread out his jacket, creating a makeshift blanket. Shannon looked at him, her cheeks flushed, and he felt a rush of desire.

"Are you sure?" he asked, his heart pounding. He wanted to cherish this moment, to make it unforgettable.

"I'm sure," she replied, her voice steady and full of love. "I trust you, Gavin."

As they lay together beneath the branches, the sounds of nature enveloped them. Their kisses grew more passionate, hands exploring with a reverence that spoke of their deepening bond. Gavin felt as if they were the only two people in the world, lost in each other, their hearts beating in perfect harmony.

Time slipped away, and the sun began to set, casting a soft light around them. When they finally found their release, it was as if the world exploded in color—an explosion of joy, love, and connection. They lay entwined in each other's arms, the world around them fading as they basked in the afterglow of their love.

Shannon shifted slightly, propping herself up on her elbow, a contemplative look on her face. Gavin brushed a strand of hair from her cheek, his heart swelling at the sight of her.

Gavin smiled softly as he traced his fingers along her jawline, his touch gentle, reverent. "What are you thinking?" he asked, his voice low and warm, still tinged with the passion of their shared moment.

Shannon's gaze met his, her hazel eyes shimmering in the soft twilight. "I'm thinking... this feels like a dream," she admitted, her voice barely above a whisper. "Like something I don't deserve but never want to let go of."

Gavin cupped her cheek, his thumb brushing over her freckles. "You deserve everything, Shannon," he said earnestly. "Every happiness, every joy. I'd give it all to you if I could."

She smiled, her lips trembling slightly, and leaned into his touch. "You already have, Gavin. I don't think I've ever felt more… alive than I do right now."

They lay there for a while in peaceful silence, the meadow around them alive with the soft hum of crickets and the gentle rustling of the tall grass in the evening breeze. The world seemed vast, yet intimate, as if it existed solely for them in that fleeting moment.

Gavin shifted onto his back, pulling Shannon with him so she rested her head on his chest. She traced lazy patterns across his skin, the rhythm of his heartbeat steady beneath her touch.

"Do you think it'll always be like this?" she asked quietly, her voice tinged with both hope and uncertainty.

Gavin pressed a kiss to the top of her head, inhaling the faint scent of wild flowers in her hair. "I don't know what the future holds," he admitted, "but I know I'll fight for this. For you. For us."

Shannon's fingers stilled against his chest as she lifted her head to look at him. "Promise me something," she said, her tone serious now.

"Anything," he said without hesitation.

"Promise me that no matter what happens, you won't ever regret this," she said, her voice steady but her eyes searching his face for reassurance.

Gavin reached up, cradling her face in both hands. "Shannon, there isn't a force on this earth that could make me regret loving you," he said firmly.

A tear slipped down her cheek, and he brushed it away with his thumb. She leaned down, their lips meeting in a kiss that was slow and tender, filled with a love that words could never fully capture.

The warmth of the day began to fade as the evening settled over the meadow. Gavin and Shannon lay tangled together, the grass soft beneath them, a blanket of stars slowly emerging overhead. The world around them grew quieter, the hum of insects replaced by the distant calls of night birds and the occasional rustle of the wind through the trees.

Gavin absently ran his fingers along Shannon's arm, tracing the curve of her shoulder and the delicate line of her collarbone. She nestled against him, her cheek resting on his chest, her breath soft and even. The connection between them felt unshakable, as if the world itself had paused to give them this sacred moment.

"Do you think they'll notice I've been gone this long?" Shannon murmured, her voice laced with a mixture of humor and worry.

Gavin chuckled, the sound low and comforting. "Not unless they've been keeping time by the stars," he teased, pressing a kiss to the top of her head. "But we should probably head back soon. I don't want anyone thinking I've stolen you away for good."

Shannon smiled, though her reluctance to leave was clear. "Maybe I wouldn't mind if you did," she said softly, her words carrying a weight that hung between them like a secret.

Gavin lifted her chin gently, his eyes meeting hers. "One day," he said, his voice filled with quiet determination. "But for now, I'll settle for making sure you get home safely."

Reluctantly, they untangled themselves, the cool evening air brushing against their bare skin. Gavin helped Shannon gather her dress, brushing stray blades of grass from the fabric before pulling her into one last embrace. She laughed softly, her arms circling his waist as they stood there, reluctant to part even for a moment.

As the evening deepened, Shannon held Gavin close as the pair rode back toward the edge of the meadow, their fingers entwined. The path home felt longer in the stillness of the evening, the faint glow of lanterns from the town ahead acting as their guide.

When they reached the road near Shannon's home, they stopped beneath the shadow of a tall oak tree. Gavin turned to her, his gaze lingering as if trying to memorize every detail of her face. "Goodnight, Shannon," he said softly, his voice carrying both a farewell and a promise.

"Goodnight, Gavin," she replied, her voice barely above a whisper.

He leaned down, pressing a lingering kiss to her lips before stepping back. Shannon watched him until he disappeared into the shadows, her heart full yet aching at the thought of leaving him. As she turned toward her home, her steps light but her thoughts heavy, she knew that what they had shared that day had changed everything.

Gavin rode his horse through the quiet streets of Maple Creek that night. The lanterns hanging from the store fronts cast flickering pools of light on the dirt road, and the faint sounds of laughter and conversation spilled from the saloon. Gavin's mind was still on Shannon, her touch, her smile, the way her laughter lingered in the air like a melody he never wanted to forget.

As he guided his horse past the general store, a figure stepped out from the shadows of the alley. "You must be Gavin Craite," a low, mocking voice called out.

Gavin slowed his horse, his sharp eyes narrowing as he took in the man standing before him. He was stocky, with a swaggering stance and an expression that reeked of trouble.

"I might be," Gavin said coolly, his tone calm but edged with a quiet authority. He tilted his hat slightly, his gaze steady and unreadable. "And who might you be?"

"Ellis Grady," the man said, his lips curling into a sneer. "I've heard a lot about you."

Gavin remained silent; his composure unshaken. He dismounted slowly, his boots hitting the ground with a deliberate thud. If Ellis wanted to size him up, he wasn't going to do it while Gavin was on horseback.

Ellis stepped closer, invading Gavin's space, his grin turning nastier. "You've been spending a lot of time with Shannon McAllister, haven't you? You think you're somethin' special?"

Gavin's jaw tightened ever so slightly, but his expression remained calm. "Shannon's choices are her own," he said evenly. "If you've got a problem with her, I suggest you get over it."

Ellis let out a bitter laugh. "She and I had something special you know. I just wasn't ready to settle down just yet. Needed to get some experience out of my system. Not sure what she's doing hanging around with you for." He leaned in closer, his voice dropping to a menacing growl. "Let me give you some advice: stay away from her. I don't take kindly to others sampling what's mine."

Gavin's gaze didn't waver. He didn't flinch, didn't react. Instead, he took a deliberate step forward, forcing Ellis to take a step back. "I don't take kindly to being told what to do. Furthermore, Shannon is free to do as she wishes and it would seem what she wishes for right now, ain't you," Gavin said softly, his voice like steel wrapped in velvet. "If you've got something to say, say it straight. Otherwise, step aside."

The tension between them was electric, the kind

of standoff that drew attention even in the stillness of the night. Several townsfolk peeked out of windows and doorways, sensing the brewing conflict.

Just as Ellis's hand twitched toward his belt, a deep voice cut through the tension. "That's enough!"

Both men turned to see Sheriff Bill Grady approaching, his star glinting in the lamplight. His broad shoulders and weathered face carried the authority of a man who'd seen his fair share of trouble—and knew how to put an end to it.

"Ellis," Bill said sharply, his eyes narrowing at his son. "What in God's name do you think you're doing, son?"

"Just having a chat with our new friend here," Ellis said, his voice dripping with false innocence.

"Doesn't look like much of a chat to me," the sheriff replied, his tone cold. He turned to Gavin, giving him a once-over. "You alright, mister?"

Gavin nodded, his hand resting casually on his belt, though his posture remained alert. "I'm fine, Sheriff. Just a misunderstanding."

Bill's eyes flicked back to Ellis, his expression hardening. "It's late, head on back home, now."

Ellis hesitated, glaring at Gavin for a long moment before spitting on the ground. "This ain't over," he muttered, stalking off into the shadows.

Bill sighed, tipping his hat toward Gavin. "Apologies for my son. He's got more temper than sense."

"No harm done," Gavin replied, his tone polite but distant.

The sheriff gave him a long look before nodding. "You take care now," he said, turning on his heel and walking away.

As Gavin mounted his horse and rode off, he couldn't help but feel the calamity of the encounter lingering in the air. Trouble had a way of following men like Ellis, and Gavin knew this wouldn't be the last time their paths crossed. But for now, his thoughts were on Shannon and the promise of what lay ahead.

CHAPTER 8

The golden hues of late autumn stretched across the landscape, the farm basking in the warmth of the fading sun. Gavin and Shannon had spent the afternoon together, tending to the small vegetable garden behind the Craite house. Shannon's laughter had filled the air as Gavin teased her about her gardening skills—or lack thereof.

"Maybe if you didn't uproot the carrots with such enthusiasm, we'd have more of them," he said, grinning as he held up a lopsided, half-broken carrot.

Shannon swatted at him with her gloves, a playful glint in her eyes. "Maybe if you spent less time talking and more time working, we'd finish before sundown."

The ease between them felt natural, like they'd known each other their whole lives. Their love had deepened over the past few months, a bond forged not just through passion but through quiet moments like these.

As the evening began to settle in, Shannon grew quiet. Her hands worked methodically, but her gaze seemed distant, her usual lightheartedness replaced with a pensive expression. Gavin noticed but didn't press her, knowing she'd speak when she was ready.

After the garden was finished, they walked hand in hand to the porch, the cool breeze carrying the scent of the coming winter. Gavin fetched two mugs of tea from the kitchen, handing one to Shannon as they sat side by side on the steps.

Shannon cradled the warm mug in her hands, staring out at the horizon where the sun dipped below the treetops. Gavin leaned back, content in the silence, though he couldn't shake the feeling that something was on her mind.

"Gavin," she began, her voice soft, almost hesitant.

He straightened, setting his mug down and turning to face her. "What is it, love?"

She took a deep breath, her fingers tightening around the mug. "I've been feeling… different lately. Tired, a little queasy in the mornings." She glanced at him, her eyes searching his face.

He frowned, concern knitting his brow. "You're not sick, are you? Should we get Doc Morrow to—"

"No," she interrupted, shaking her head. "It's not that." She hesitated, as if trying to find the right words. "Gavin… I think… I think I might be pregnant."

The words hung in the air, and for a moment, time

stood still. Gavin's heart raced as he processed her words.

"Are you sure?" he asked, concern etched on his face.

"I haven't had my cycle," she replied, biting her lip. "I didn't want to say anything until I was certain, but I feel it in my bones."

Gavin's heart soared and plummeted simultaneously, a whirlwind of emotions crashing over him. "Shannon, this is… incredible. I mean, it's a lot, but… it means everything."

"Are you… are you okay with this?" she asked, her eyes searching his.

"More than okay," he said, his voice firm. "I want to spend the rest of my life with you and our child."

Taking a deep breath, Gavin reached into his pocket, his heart pounding as he pulled out a small, weathered piece of cloth. Inside lay a simple silver ring that had belonged to his mother—a token of love and commitment.

"Shannon," he said, his voice steady but filled with emotion, "will you marry me?"

Her eyes widened in surprise, then filled with tears as she nodded vigorously. "Yes! Yes, a thousand times, yes!"

Gavin had gone into his mother's drawer a while back and had carried her wedding ring in his pocket for just such a moment. Gavin slipped the ring onto her finger, a perfect fit that symbolized their love and commitment. They kissed again, sealing their promise beneath the ancient oak tree, surrounded by the beauty of the land they would one day call home.

As the sun dipped below the horizon, coloring the sky pink and gold, they knew that their whirlwind romance had only just begun. Their love story was unfolding like the wildflowers blooming around them, filled with promise and the hope of a bright future.

CHAPTER 9

Night was rolling in and the fading sun was shining its last brilliance on the secluded trail that wound its way from town to Gavin's farm. The vibrant colors of the wildflowers lining the path danced in the gentle breeze, but the peaceful scene belied the darkness that loomed nearby.

Gavin and Shannon walked hand in hand, their laughter echoing in the stillness of the evening, oblivious to the danger lurking just out of sight. They had stolen away from town, seeking a moment of solitude, a chance to revel in their love away from prying eyes.

But as they rounded a bend in the trail, the atmosphere shifted. Gavin felt a tingle of unease prick at the back of his neck. The laughter faded from Shannon's lips as she sensed the change.

"Gavin, do you hear that?" she asked, her voice barely above a whisper.

Before he could respond, a group of figures emerged from the trees, blocking their path. It was Ellis, flanked by three other men, a predatory smile spreading across his face. The tension in the air thickened, turning the warm summer evening cold.

"Well, well, what do we have here?" Ellis drawled, his voice dripping with malice. "A couple of lovebirds lost in the woods?"

Gavin's heart raced as he stepped protectively in front of Shannon, his fists clenching at his sides. "What do you want, Ellis?" he demanded, trying to keep his voice steady.

"I just want to have a little chat with you, Craite," Ellis replied, stepping closer, his friends flanking him like wolves closing in on their prey. "You've been spending too much time with my girl."

"Shannon is not yours," Gavin shot back, feeling the adrenaline rush through him. "You lost her the moment you laid a hand on her."

"Such brave words," Ellis sneered, his eyes narrowing. "But let's see how brave you really are."

Before Gavin could react, Ellis lunged at him, fists flying. Gavin instinctively fought back, throwing punches, but the other men swarmed him, their hands grabbing him from behind and dragging him to the ground. He struggled, kicking and thrashing, but they were too strong.

"Get off me!" Gavin shouted, but his words were drowned out by the roar of laughter from Ellis and his cronies. They held him down, pinning his arms to the ground as he fought against their grip.

"Just teachin' you a lesson," Ellis said, his voice cold and menacing. "You should've stayed away from her."

Gavin felt the world spin as one of Ellis's friends landed a punch to his stomach, knocking the wind out of him. Stars danced in his vision as he gasped for breath, but he fought to stay conscious, desperate to protect Shannon.

"Shannon, run!" he managed to croak, but she was frozen in fear, her eyes wide with terror.

But Ellis was too quick. "Don't even think about it, darling," he said, taking a step toward her. "You and I started a dance we never got to finish, remember?"

Panic surged through Gavin as he watched Ellis approach Shannon, the fear in her eyes cutting deeper than any physical blow. "Get away from her!" he screamed, but the grip of Ellis's friends tightened, holding him down, rendering him helpless.

Shannon took a step back, her voice shaking. "Please, Ellis, don't do this."

"Oh, but I have to," he said, his smile twisted. "You think you can just leave me? Tsk, tsk, I won't let that happen."

Gavin fought harder, rage boiling inside him as he watched helplessly. Ellis closed the distance, his intentions clear, and Gavin's heart shattered with the realization of what was about to happen.

In that moment, the world faded into a blur of

sounds and screams, darkness closing in on Gavin as he struggled against the suffocating weight of his captors.

Gavin awoke to the sound of muffled cries, the world spinning as he tried to sit up. His body ached, and confusion clouded his mind. As he blinked against the bright light, he noticed Shannon crouched nearby, her back to him, shaking uncontrollably.

"Shannon?" he croaked, his throat dry and raw.

She turned, and the sight that met his eyes tore through him like a dagger. Her clothes were torn, bruises blossoming on her skin, her eyes filled with fear and anguish. The sight of her like this sent waves of despair crashing over him.

"Gavin…" she gasped, tears streaming down her cheeks. "I'm so sorry…"

"What happened?" he asked, panic flooding his veins. He struggled to push himself up, but his limbs felt heavy, as if weighed down by lead. "What did he do to you?"

Shannon crumpled to the ground, her sobs breaking Gavin's heart. "Ellis… he—he hurt me. I tried to fight him off, but… he had his way with me."

The words hung in the air, and Gavin felt his world shatter around him. Anger, guilt, and helplessness consumed him, a tempest of emotions threatening to consume him whole.

"Where is he?" Gavin demanded, struggling to regain his footing. "I'll make him pay for this!"

"Gavin, please," Shannon cried, reaching for him,

her eyes pleading. "You can't. He's gone. I don't want you to get hurt too."

Gavin felt rage boiling inside him, his fists clenched tightly as he fought against the pain and confusion. He wanted nothing more than to take her in his arms, to shield her from the horrors she had endured, but the reality of their situation loomed heavy over them.

"I'm so sorry, Shannon," he said, his voice breaking. "I couldn't stop him."

Tears streamed down her face as she shook her head. "It's not your fault, Gavin. I was so scared. I didn't know what to do."

Gavin pulled her into his arms, holding her tightly as she cried against him, their bodies trembling with the gravity of their trauma. In that moment, he vowed to himself that he would never let anyone hurt her again.

But as the sun began to set on the horizon, painting the sky with shades of red and orange, Gavin felt an overwhelming sense of loss wash over him. The future they had envisioned together now felt tainted, overshadowed by the darkness that had invaded their lives.

They were changed forever, and as they held each other in the fading light, the reality of their situation settled like a heavy blanket over them, a chilling reminder of the battle they would have to face together.

CHAPTER 10

Time went by, Gavin began to heal from the injuries he sustained from Ellis' cohorts in the attack. However, the emotional damage caused by the atrocity Ellis served upon Shannon would never heal. Gavin's heart raced as he paced the floor of his dimly lit cabin, the weight of the world pressing down on him. The evening air was thick with the scent of pine and the smoke from the fireplace, but all he could smell was the bitterness of anger and betrayal.

Shannon sat quietly at the small table, her hands clasped tightly in her lap, her expression a mixture of concern and fear. "Gavin, please… you need to think this through," she pleaded, her voice soft yet firm. "Ellis is dangerous. His father is the sheriff. You'll only make things worse."

Gavin stopped and turned to face her; the firelight casting shadows across his rugged face. "What he did to you, Shannon… it's unforgivable. I can't just sit back and let him get away with it. He needs to pay."

Tears glistened in Shannon's eyes, and she stood up, moving closer to him. "But revenge won't change what happened. It won't take away the pain. It'll only put you in danger. I can't lose you too."

Gavin clenched his fists, the memory of that night flooding back to him—Shannon's cries, the look of fear on her face as Ellis closed in on her. The image was burned into his mind, fueling the fire of his resolve. "I have to do this," he said, his voice low and filled with determination. "I can't let him think he can just walk away."

Shannon stepped back, her expression shifting from pleading to despair. "You're not a killer, Gavin. This isn't you. You're better than this."

"Better than what?" he shot back, the anger boiling over. "Better than standing up for the woman I love? Better than protecting my family? He's a monster, Shannon, and monsters don't deserve mercy."

Silence hung between them, heavy and suffocating. Gavin could see the pain in Shannon's eyes, the conflict that tore at her heart. She wanted to keep him safe, to protect him from the darkness that was threatening to consume him. But in that moment, all Gavin could see was red.

As night fell, Gavin slipped out of the cabin, the cool air brushing against his skin. He moved through the trees like a shadow, driven by a singular purpose.

The world around him faded away; all that mattered was the reckoning he had set in motion.

Gavin went in search of Ellis. He had heard the rumors—Ellis was at the saloon, no doubt bragging to whomever would listen about his conquest over Shannon. As he approached, the sounds of raucous laughter and clinking glasses filled the air, but Gavin was undeterred. He would not let Ellis hide behind the safety of his friends tonight.

Gavin stepped inside the saloon, his gaze locking onto Ellis, who sat slumped at the bar, a bottle of whiskey in hand. The sight of him twisted Gavin's gut, a mixture of rage and satisfaction coursing through him. This was it.

"Ellis," he called out, his voice cutting through the noise like a knife.

Ellis looked up, surprise flickering in his eyes, quickly replaced by a sneer. "Well, well, if it isn't the little hero. Come to join me for a drink?"

Gavin's fists tightened at his sides. "No, I came to settle things once and for all."

Ellis's laughter rang hollow as he stood, swaying slightly. "You think you can take me on? You're outnumbered, Craite."

"Are you too afraid to take me on yourself? You need to hide behind these men? I'm not afraid of you Ellis. Are you afraid of me?" Gavin shot back, stepping closer, the air thick with tension. "What you did to Shannon... I'm not going to let you get away with it."

In an instant, the laughter in the saloon faded, eyes turning to the confrontation unfolding before them. Ellis's friends shifted uncomfortably, sensing the impending violence.

"You think you're tough, huh? You think you can just waltz in here and make threats?" Ellis taunted, stepping closer. "You don't know what I'm capable of. Do you even know who my father is? I run this town."

Gavin's patience snapped. He lunged at Ellis, landing a powerful punch that sent him staggering backward. The saloon erupted in chaos as people scrambled back, but Gavin didn't care. He was a whirlwind of fury, throwing punches, driven by the memory of Shannon's tears.

Ellis fought back, but he was no match for Gavin's strength, which was fueled with rage. With each blow, Gavin felt his pain lift, replaced by a sense of purpose. He tackled Ellis to the ground, the wood floor creaking beneath their struggle, fists connecting with flesh in a blur of violence.

"Don't you ever touch her again!" Gavin shouted, his voice raw as he landed another blow, his heart racing with adrenaline.

Ellis groaned, struggling to get his bearings. "You'll pay for this, Craite," he spat, his face bruised and bloodied. "You don't know who you're messing with. My father will—"

"Your father?" Gavin interrupted, his voice low and dangerous. "He doesn't scare me. You're nothing but a coward hiding behind his badge."

With a final eruption of strength, Gavin pinned Ellis to the ground, his hands wrapped around his throat. The world around them faded away, leaving only the two of them in that moment—a confrontation long overdue.

"Now you listen to me," Gavin growled, his voice steady. "You threaten Shannon again, and I swear I will end you."

As he released his grip, Gavin stood, breathing heavily as Ellis gasped for air, fury etched across his bruised face. But as Gavin turned to leave, he heard Ellis's voice, low and menacing.

"She loved it you know; she was moaning like a whore with every inch I put inside of her."

Gavin's blood ran cold, and in an instant, the world narrowed down to a single thought. Ellis will hang for this injustice.

He glanced around, the saloon was quiet. All eyes locking onto Gavin and Ellis. Gavin knew he couldn't do what needed doing in the saloon. He'd be strung up just for trying. It was a crude reminder of the lawlessness that lurked beneath the surface of their small town, and Gavin knew what he had to do.

He turned back to Ellis, who was struggling to rise. "You're a dead man," Gavin said, his voice cold and unwavering. "And I'm going to make sure you never hurt her again."

As Gavin walked out of the saloon, he heard Ellis

calling after him "run away you little coward. I'll find you."

"Sooner than you think Ellis." Gavin muttered to himself as he mounted his horse.

Gavin rode a short way down the street and waited for Ellis to leave the saloon. It took about 30 minutes or so before he saw Ellis stumbling out of the bar on his own. Without thinking twice Gavin rode up beside. "Looks like you found me."

Gavin roped Ellis around the torso and dragged him out of town into the moonlit night, the cool air biting against his skin. The stars glimmered above, but they felt distant and indifferent to the violence that was about to unfold. He could hear Ellis's ragged breathing behind him, the reality of what he was about to do weighing heavily on his conscience.

"Please, Gavin, don't do this!" Ellis pleaded, panic creeping into his voice. "You don't have to—"

"Shut up," Gavin snapped, tying the rope around Ellis's neck with swift, practiced movements. "You've had your chance."

Ellis's eyes widened in fear, and he struggled against Gavin's grip. "You're making a mistake! You can't do this! My father—"

"Your father ain't here to save you," Gavin said, his voice steady and resolute. "You think you can take what you want from the people I love and walk away without consequences?"

Blinded by rage, Gavin threw the other end of the

rope over a branch then yanked the rope tight, the world around them falling silent. In that moment, he felt a mix of power and dread, knowing he was crossing a line he could never uncross. But what Ellis had done was too much, a wound too deep to ignore.

Gavin stepped back, watching as Ellis struggled, fear etched across his face. He knew this was a choice he could never take back, but in that moment, it felt like the only option left.

The moon shone down on them, illuminating the darkness that surrounded their lives. And as Ellis' struggles grew weaker, Gavin felt a mixture of relief and horror wash over him. He had exacted his revenge, but at what cost?

As Ellis's body went limp, Gavin turned away, the seriousness of his actions settling heavily on his shoulders. He had crossed into darkness, a place where love and revenge blurred together. And now, as he walked away from the tree, he knew that nothing would ever be the same.

The night air was still, but within Gavin, a storm raged. He had avenged Shannon, but the victory felt hollow, tainted by the darkness that had taken root in his heart. He could only hope that, in time, they could find a way to heal from the wounds that would forever mark their lives.

CHAPTER 11

The night sky stretched overhead, dark and endless, as Gavin made his way back to the cabin. Each step felt heavier than the last, as if the weight of what he'd done was dragging him into the earth. The pine trees rustled in the wind, whispering their secrets, but Gavin could only hear the echo of Ellis' final gasps. The taste of vengeance still lingered bitterly in his mouth, and he wasn't sure how to face Shannon.

When the homestead came into view, warm light spilling from the windows, his heart clenched. Inside, Shannon was waiting, but she had no idea how everything had changed.

He pushed open the door gently. Shannon sat at the table; her face illumining by the flickering glow of the oil lamp. Her dark hair fell around her shoulders, and for a moment, just a moment, Gavin wanted to forget everything and lose himself in her presence.

But he couldn't. Not now.

She looked up at him, a small smile tugging at her lips, but it faded quickly when she saw the haunted look in his eyes.

"Gavin," she whispered, standing and crossing the room to him. "What happened? Are you alright?"

He couldn't meet her eyes, not at first. The blood on his knuckles had dried, and the grime of the night's violence clung to his skin. "I... I did something, Shannon."

Her face dropped in concern as she reached out to touch his face, but he flinched away. He couldn't let her see him like this, broken and tainted by what he'd done.

"Gavin," she said softly, her voice trembling, "what did you do?"

He took a deep breath, his chest tight with the burden of his actions. He had hoped he wouldn't have to tell her, that somehow, he could leave without burdening her with the truth. But she deserved to know.

"I found Ellis," he said, his voice rough. "I confronted him... And I... I killed him."

Shannon's eyes widened in shock, her hand covering her mouth as she stumbled back. "Gavin... no."

"I had to," he said quickly, his words tumbling out in a rush. "He threatened you, Shannon. After everything he did, he said he'd never leave you alone. I couldn't let that happen."

Tears welled up in her eyes as she shook her head, trying to process the horror of it all. "Don't you put this on me…But his father… Gavin, Bill's the sheriff. He'll come after you."

"I know," Gavin said, his voice heavy with resignation. "That's why I have to leave. Tonight."

"No…" Shannon's voice cracked, and she took a step toward him, desperation in her eyes. "You can't leave. We'll find a way—"

"There's no way out of this, Shannon," Gavin interrupted, his voice firm but filled with sorrow. "Bill will hunt me down. He'll make sure I swing for this. I've bought us some time, but he'll know soon enough. I have to go."

Shannon's tears fell freely now, and she reached for him, pulling him into a fierce embrace. Gavin closed his eyes, breathing in the familiar scent of her hair, the warmth of her body pressed against his. It took everything in him not to break down, but he had to be strong. For both of them.

"How long?" she whispered, her voice barely audible.

"I don't know," he admitted. "But I promise I'll come back for you. I'll find a way."

Shannon pulled back just enough to look up at him, her tear-streaked face filled with a mixture of hope and despair. "Don't make promises you can't keep, Gavin."

"I'll keep this one," he said, his voice steady. "I swear it. I'll come back for you. And when I do, we'll leave this place behind. We'll start over somewhere new. Somewhere safe."

The words felt hollow even as he said them, but he wanted—needed—her to believe them. Because if she didn't, then there was no point in him running.

Shannon reached up, cupping his face in her hands, her thumbs brushing against his scarred cheek. "I love you, Gavin. More than anything."

"I love you too," he whispered, his voice breaking. "That's why I have to go. To keep you safe."

They stood there for what felt like an eternity, wrapped in each other's arms, the weight of the world pressing down on them. Neither of them wanted to let go, but they both knew this was goodbye. Maybe not forever, but for now.

Finally, Shannon leaned up, pressing her lips to his in a kiss that was slow, deep, and filled with all the unspoken words they couldn't say. It was a kiss of longing, of sorrow, of promises that might never be fulfilled. Gavin's hands held her tightly, trying to memorize every curve, every touch, as if he could carry her with him wherever he went.

When they pulled apart, the world felt colder, emptier.

"Go," Shannon said softly, her voice trembling. "Before it's too late."

Gavin nodded, his heart aching as he stepped back.

He grabbed his worn leather coat, slung it over his shoulder, and gave her one last look. Her tear-filled eyes shone in the lamplight, and he burned the image of her standing there, bathed in that soft glow, into his memory.

"Stay safe," he said, his voice barely above a whisper. "I'll come back for you."

Shannon nodded, her lips trembling. "I'll be waiting."

With that, Gavin turned and left the cabin, the door closing softly behind him. He didn't look back, because if he did, he wasn't sure he'd be able to leave.

The night air was crisp as he stepped into the darkness, his heart heavy with the knowledge that he was leaving behind the only person he'd ever truly loved. But it was the only way. Ellis' death had set things in motion that he couldn't stop, and now, all he could do was run.

He'd come back for her. Someday.

But for now, Gavin Craite was a man on the run.

CHAPTER 12

The mountains loomed high above Gavin as he crouched beneath a thicket of pines, the chill of the night air seeping into his bones. Shadows danced across the rocky terrain, the moonlight filtering through the branches, casting an ethereal glow that made the world seem both beautiful and haunting. It was a world he had once roamed freely with dreams in his heart, but now, every rustle of the wind felt like a reminder of his past and the darkness that had consumed him.

For days, he had stayed hidden, avoiding the roads and trails he once knew like the back of his hand. He had been running ever since the night he had taken Ellis' life, a violent act that had shattered everything he held dear. His heart ached with every memory of Shannon, her laughter echoing in his mind like a song he couldn't forget.

Gavin's stomach growled, a painful reminder of his hunger, but he had no desire to leave his hiding place. He feared that if he ventured down the mountain, he might find himself face to face with the posse searching for him, or worse, that his capture would mean leaving Shannon and their unborn child to fend for themselves.

The sound of distant hoofbeats snapped him out of his thoughts. He froze, gripping the handle of his knife instinctively. He pressed himself closer to the ground, his breath shallow as the rhythmic thudding grew louder, echoing off the rocky crags.

Through the veil of pine branches, he caught sight of a lone figure on horseback. The rider moved cautiously, his posture relaxed yet alert, as if aware of the dangers lurking in these mountains. As the horse drew closer, Gavin's grip on his knife eased. He recognized the broad shoulders and steady hands on the reins.

"Marek," he whispered to himself, relief washing over him.

Marek dismounted a few yards away, scanning the area before calling out softly, "Gavin? You here, brother?"

Gavin stepped out from the shadows, his lean frame gaunt and his clothes worn from days of rough living. "Marek," he said, his voice low but steady.

Marek turned, his eyes narrowing as they took in Gavin's appearance. "You look like hell," he muttered, tossing a sack to the ground between them. "Figured you'd need food. Got some jerky, bread, and a flask of water in there. And a little coin."

Gavin nodded, crouching to open the sack. He pulled out a strip of jerky, chewing slowly as he watched Marek with a wary gratitude. "Thank you."

Marek sighed, leaning against his horse. "The posse's still combing the woods, but they're scattered. Bill's got them worked up, and half of them don't even know what they're looking for. I slipped away when I could."

Gavin swallowed; Marek's words settling heavily on his shoulders. "How's Shannon?" he asked, his voice quieter now, almost trembling.

"She's holding up," Marek replied. "Worried sick about you, though. She's staying with us at the farm for now. Her Pa threw her out when she told him of the pregnancy, what with her not being wed and all. She hasn't told anyone about…" He trailed off, gesturing vaguely. "You know what happened with Ellis."

Gavin nodded, staring out at the dark horizon. "Good. She doesn't need more trouble right now."

Marek stepped closer, his expression stern. "What's your plan, Gavin? You can't just live out here forever."

"I don't plan to," Gavin said firmly. "I'll stay hidden until Shannon's had the baby. Once she's ready, we'll leave. Head west or south, anywhere but here. Start over."

Marek frowned. "And you think Bill Grady's just

going to let that happen? He won't stop looking for you, Gavin. Killing his boy... that's not something he's going to forgive."

"I didn't have a choice," Gavin shot back, his voice hardening. "Ellis was going to hurt Shannon. You think I could just stand there and let that happen?"

Marek raised his hands in a placating gesture. "I'm not saying you were wrong. But you know how Bill is. He doesn't care about the why, just the what."

The brothers stood in silence for a moment, the tension between them softened only by the quiet rustling of the trees.

"You should go," Gavin finally said, his tone softer. "If they see you're missing, they'll start asking questions."

Marek hesitated, then reached into his pocket and pulled out a folded piece of paper. "Here," he said, handing it to Gavin. "It's a map of the area. Marked some spots where you can lay low if you have to move."

Gavin took the map, his fingers brushing against Marek's for a moment. "Thank you," he said, his voice thick with emotion.

Marek swung back onto his horse, looking down at his brother with a mixture of worry and resolve. "Stay safe, Gavin. And if you need anything, you know where to find me."

Gavin nodded, watching as Marek rode off into the darkness. Once the sound of hoofbeats faded into the night, he unfolded the map and studied it in the pale moonlight, committing the marks to memory.

He knew the road ahead would be long and fraught with danger, but his resolve was unwavering. For Shannon, for their child, and for the promise of a life far away from the chaos he had left behind, Gavin would endure.

Over the next few months, Marek became Gavin's lifeline, a solitary thread connecting him to the world he had been forced to leave behind. The treks to Gavin's hideout were long and perilous, with the threat of discovery always looming, but Marek made the journey without complaint. He knew his brother's survival depended on it.

Each trip began in the dead of night, Marek leaving the Craite homestead under the guise of tending to far-off chores or hunting game. With a sack of supplies slung over his shoulder and a pistol tucked into his belt, he would ride deep into the mountains, his horse navigating the rugged terrain with practiced ease.

Gavin was always waiting, his lean figure emerging from the shadows as soon as he heard Marek's approach. The brothers would exchange a brief nod before Marek handed over the provisions: bread, smoked meat, and occasionally something fresh, like apples or a flask of soup Marek had smuggled out of the house.

"How's Shannon?" Gavin would ask every time, the question almost a ritual.

"She's holding up," Marek would reply, sometimes with more detail. "She's been staying busy with sewing and helping around the farm, mending things, keeping the house, doing chores. She's strong, Gavin. But she misses you."

The updates were Gavin's lifeline to hope. Marek told him about the small victories Shannon experienced—how she'd finished a quilt for the baby or how she would sit in her rocking-chair singing lullabies looking out the window.. Every story, no matter how small, painted a picture of the life Gavin was fighting to return to.

But there were harder truths, too. Marek didn't sugar coat the realities of the situation. The posse hadn't given up; Bill Grady was relentless, riding out regularly with men to search the mountains. "They're frustrated," Marek admitted one night as they sat around a small fire. "They think you've gone farther south. But they're still out there."

Gavin listened in silence, his face a mask of determination. He knew the risk he was taking by staying so close, but he couldn't bring himself to leave. Not until Shannon and the baby were ready to join him.

On one trip, Marek brought a letter. "From Shannon," he said, pulling it from his pocket. "She couldn't risk anyone seeing her give it to me, so she wrote it late at night."

Gavin's hands trembled as he took the folded

paper. He read it by the light of the fire, Shannon's words filling him with equal parts joy and heartbreak. She wrote about her dreams for their future, her faith in him, and her undying love. She ended the letter with a promise: "*No matter what happens, we'll find our way back to each other.*"

"I'll get us there," Gavin murmured to himself, folding the letter and tucking it into his shirt.

As the weeks turned into months, Marek noticed the toll the isolation was taking on his brother. Gavin's face grew leaner, his eyes more haunted, though his resolve never wavered. Marek tried to lift his spirits, bringing small comforts like a deck of cards or a flask of whiskey. They talked about their childhood, the old days on the farm, and dreams they once shared.

"Do you think I'll make it out of this, Marek?" Gavin asked one night, his voice barely audible over the crackle of the fire.

Marek didn't answer immediately. He stared into the flames, the uncertainty of the question pressing heavily on him. "I don't know," he admitted finally. "But I do know this: you're not alone in this. We'll get through it, somehow."

It wasn't the reassurance Gavin had hoped for, but it was enough.

As the days grew shorter and the air colder, Marek continued his journeys, always careful, always alert. Each time he left, he carried the same prayer in his heart: that he would find Gavin alive and safe on his next visit, and that one day, the visits wouldn't be necessary at all.

Marek's ride home was slow and steady, the responsibi of his secret pressing down on him as much as the supplies he carried back and forth from the mountains. The chill of the evening air nipped at his face, and his horse's hooves clopped rhythmically against the rocky path. He was careful, as always, to take a different route each time, ensuring no one could easily track his movements.

But this night, his precautions weren't enough.

The sound of galloping hooves cut through the stillness, and Marek's heart sank as he saw the familiar silhouette of Sheriff Bill Grady astride his horse. The sheriff raised a hand, signaling Marek to stop.

"Well, if it isn't Marek Craite," Bill drawled, his voice cold and measured. His sharp eyes scanned Marek and the contents of his saddlebag. "Out late, aren't you? Carrying some empty bags? Dropping supplies off for someone, maybe?"

"Just hunting," Marek replied, keeping his tone even. "Keeping them empty in case I caught something, which I didn't. Winter's coming, you know."

"Hunting," Bill repeated, dismounting his horse and taking a step closer. His boots crunched against the dirt. "Funny, I've been hearing stories about someone sneaking up into the mountains, bringing food and such. Sounded an awful lot like you."

Marek's grip on the reins tightened, but he kept his

expression neutral. "I don't know what you're talking about, Sheriff. I've got a family to look after, same as anyone else."

Bill's jaw tightened, his patience wearing thin. "Don't play dumb with me, Marek. You've been running supplies to your brother, haven't you? Where is he?"

"I don't know where Gavin is," Marek lied, his voice steady. "Haven't seen him since the night he ran."

Bill studied him for a long moment, the silence between them thick with tension. Then, without warning, the sheriff lashed out, his fist connecting with Marek's jaw. The force of the blow knocked Marek off his horse, and he hit the ground hard, the taste of blood flooding his mouth.

"Where is he?" Bill demanded, towering over Marek.

Marek pushed himself up on one elbow, spitting blood into the dirt. "I told you; I don't know."

The sheriff didn't hesitate. He grabbed Marek by the collar and hauled him to his feet, delivering another punishing blow to his stomach. Marek doubled over, gasping for air, but his resolve remained unshaken.

"You think you're protecting him?" Bill hissed. "All you're doing is dragging this out. Tell me where he is, and maybe I'll let you go home tonight."

Marek straightened, wiping his bloodied lip with the back of his hand. His eyes met the sheriff's, defiant and unyielding. "You can beat me all you want, Bill.

I'm not telling you a damn thing."

Bill's face twisted with anger, and he shoved Marek back to the ground. For a moment, it seemed he might strike him again, but then he stepped away, pacing in frustration.

"You're a fool," Bill said, his voice low and dangerous. "Gavin's a dead man walking. And if you keep this up, you're going to end up in the ground right next to him."

Marek struggled to his feet, clutching his side but standing tall. "If you're done, I'd like to get home now," he said, his tone as cold as the mountain air.

Bill glared at him, his fists clenched, but after a moment, he stepped aside. "Go," he said through gritted teeth. "But this ain't over, Marek. Not by a long shot."

Marek climbed back onto his horse, his body aching but his resolve intact. He didn't look back as he rode away, the sheriff's threats echoing in his mind. He knew the danger was far from over, but he also knew one thing for certain: no matter what Bill Grady did, he wouldn't betray his brother.

***

It had been a little over a week since Marek last made the trek to visit with his brother and to bring him supplies. This trip would be a much harder journey for him. Not just because Bill Grady was onto him, but because Marek was delivering more than just supplies to Gavin. He carried with him the burden of news, news that he wasn't sure he was going to be able to give. The cold grip of night enveloped Marek as he guided his horse through the dark, moonless landscape. He relied on the feel of the reins and the steady instincts of his horse, which moved with quiet confidence through the familiar terrain. Marek had left home hours earlier, slipping away under the cover of darkness, taking winding trails and avoiding any well-trodden paths. The sheriff's threats were still fresh in his mind, and he knew this trip had to be his last.

His breath hung in the icy air as the mountain path grew steeper, the familiar scent of pine mingling with the damp earth. The silence was oppressive, broken only by the soft crunch of hooves on the ground and the occasional creak of the saddle. Marek's chest felt heavy, not just from the exertion of the ride but from the agony of the news he carried.

When he finally reached the hidden clearing where Gavin had made his camp, Marek dismounted quietly and approached the faint glow of the dying embers. Gavin sat by the fire, sharpening his knife with slow, methodical movements, his face lined with exhaustion and the grime of weeks spent in hiding. He looked up as Marek approached, his expression softening at the sight of his brother.

"You made it," Gavin said, his voice low but steady. He rose to his feet, clasping Marek's shoulder in a firm grip. "I was starting to think you weren't coming back."

"I almost didn't," Marek admitted, glancing around to ensure they were alone. He set down the small sack of supplies he'd brought, his hands lingering as if reluctant to let go.

Gavin noticed the hesitation, his brow furrowing. "What is it? What's wrong?"

Marek took a deep breath, his throat tightening as he tried to find the words. He looked at his brother, his heart aching for the man who had already lost so much. "Gavin," he began, his voice trembling, "there's no easy way to say this."

Gavin's posture stiffened, his eyes narrowing as dread crept into his expression. "Just tell me," He said, his voice barely above a whisper.

Marek swallowed hard, his gaze dropping. His hands trembled at his sides. "The baby came early, Gavin. It was… it was too soon. I tried—I swear, I tried to get her to town in time. I hitched the wagon and—she—" He choked on the words, shaking his head. "The baby…he didn't make it. Born too soon."

Gavin's face went pale. "No…"

Marek pressed on, his voice cracking under the strain of it. "She wouldn't stop bleeding. I—I did everything I could, Gavin. I held her hand… stayed with her until—"

Gavin lunged from his makeshift chair, knocking it back with a sharp scrape of wood against stone. "No! You're lying! She—she can't be—"

"She is..." Marek's voice broke, the pain raw and jagged. "I buried them, Gavin. Together down by the creek with Ma. I'm so sorry."

The words hung in the air like a thunderclap, the silence that followed deafening.

Gavin's face went pale, his hands balling into fists as he stumbled back, sinking onto a nearby log. His breath came in ragged gasps, and he pressed his hands to his face, as if trying to hold back the tidal wave of grief threatening to consume him.

"No," he whispered, shaking his head. "No, not Shannon. This can't be real. He? The baby too? Jesus." His voice cracked, and a low, guttural sound escaped him, a mix of anguish and disbelief.

Marek knelt beside him, placing a hand on his shoulder. "I'm so sorry, brother," he said softly. "I know how much she meant to you. I know how much you loved her."

Gavin lowered his hands, his eyes glistening with tears that he made no effort to hide. "She was everything," he choked out. "Everything, Marek. And now... now she's gone."

For a long time, neither of them spoke. The fire crackled softly, the only sound in the stillness of the mountains. Marek sat with his brother, giving him the only comfort he could: his presence.

Finally, Gavin spoke, his voice hollow. "I stayed here for her. For them. I thought... I thought we'd have a chance to be a family." He looked up at Marek, his expression a mixture of heartbreak and despair. "What do I do now?"

Marek met his brother's gaze, his own eyes filled with sorrow. "You survive," he said firmly. "You keep going, Gavin. For her. For the memory of the life you were building together. You don't let this destroy you."

"But I need to bury her, I need to be there to bury my family. That's my responsibility." Gavin said in a daze.

"I know, and as your brother, I will look after all of that" Marek said, his eyes pleading. "But none of that matters now. You're a wanted man. If you go back, the sheriff will see to it that you hang. You need to leave, Gavin. Get as far away as you can."

Gavin's mind raced, grappling with the pain of Marek's words. Shannon was gone. The love of his life, the light that had filled his world, was extinguished. The pain cut deeper than any knife could, and he felt hollow, a shell of the man he once was.

"Where will I go?" Gavin asked, his voice trembling. "What's left for me?"

"Anywhere but here," Marek urged, his hands gripping Gavin's shoulders, desperation evident in his gaze. "Go south, to the southern states or further, somewhere nobody will ever be looking for you . Start over. Just… don't come back. You'll only bring more pain."

Gavin's heart sank, but he knew Marek was right. There was nothing left for him in this place, nothing but ghosts and memories. "I can't believe she's gone," he murmured, the reality crashing down around him like a wave.

Marek nodded; his expression sympathetic. "I'm sorry, Gavin. I didn't want to be the one to tell you, but it's the truth. You need to go before it's too late."

With a heavy heart, Gavin stepped back, uncertainty swirling in his mind. He wanted to scream, to rage against the injustice of it all, but what good would it do? Nothing would bring Shannon back.

"Alright," he finally said, his voice barely above a whisper. "I'll leave. But I swear, if there's any chance—"

"There isn't," Marek interjected firmly. "You have to let her go. For your sake and for hers. Just promise me you'll stay safe."

Gavin nodded, tears stinging his eyes, but he refused to let them fall. He had to be strong, not just for himself but for Shannon's memory. "I promise," he said, though the words felt hollow in his mouth.

As they embraced, Gavin and Marek both felt a deep sense of loss wash over them, not just for Shannon but for the life they had once known. The bond between brothers, once unbreakable, now felt strained and fragile in the face of tragedy.

As the night wore on, Marek stayed by his brother's side, the two of them bound by grief and the unspoken promise of enduring it together.

Early he following morning, with one last look at the mountains that had sheltered him, Gavin turned away from everything he had ever known. He didn't know what awaited him in the south, but he knew he had to keep moving. The world felt cold and unforgiving, but he held on to the hope that maybe, someday, he could find a way to honor Shannon's memory.

And so, with a heavy heart and the weight of the world on his shoulders, Gavin Craite began his journey into the unknown, leaving behind the only love and life he had ever known.

CHAPTER 13

Gavin's boots kicked up dust as he walked the long, lonely stretch of dirt road, the endless horizon before him nothing but a blur of endless brown and green. He didn't know how long he'd been walking. Time had become a fading concept, tangled in a haze of regrets and painful memories. The mountains near Maple Creek were behind him now, the rugged terrain that had once felt like home now a place he could never return to. He was a man without a place, a man who'd buried his past so deeply in the soil of that place, only to have it claw its way back out, dragging him south.

He hadn't looked back since he'd left the mountains. No reason to. There was nothing there for him anymore... Shannon, who he could still feel in his bones, whose face haunted every shadow. She was gone. The baby was gone. Everything he had loved was gone, taken from him in one violent, brutal moment that had changed the course of his life forever.

Now, every step he took away from Maple Creek was a step further from the man he had been—a man who had once been whole, who had loved, who had dreamed. But those dreams had been shattered when Shannon died giving birth, and when their child died too. It was all too much, the misery of it pressing on him like the unforgiving heat of the sun above.

He couldn't go back. He couldn't face it. Not after what he'd done. He was a fugitive now, wanted for murder. The sheriff would be looking for him, the whole town of Maple Creek would be hunting him down, and they'd never stop until he was either dead or behind bars. He couldn't let that happen. Not with the memories of Shannon still fresh, not with her face still burned into his mind.

The road stretched on, winding through the hills and valleys, and Gavin kept walking, his feet sore and his body tired, but his heart weighed even heavier. He tried to keep his thoughts away from the past, but it crept back in with every step, with every long breath of dusty air.

He remembered Shannon's smile, the way her eyes had lit up when she looked at him, the way she'd held him close when the world seemed like it was too much. He remembered how they'd talked about their future, how they'd dreamed of a life together, far away from the hardships they'd known. But those dreams had died with her. And now he was alone.

The sun dipped lower in the sky, casting long shadows across the land, and Gavin kept moving, hitching rides when he could, hopping on trains when they stopped, and walking when the tracks ended. He'd never been one for much company, and the solitary nature of his journey suited him just fine. It kept him from thinking too much, kept him from feeling too much.

But there were moments—moments when he'd sit alone under the vast sky, staring at the stars, when his mind would drift back to Shannon. He could still see her face, still hear her voice in his mind, the soft way she'd laugh, the warmth of her touch. And the guilt would rise up again, thick and suffocating. He should have been there. He should have protected her. But instead, he had killed Ellis, and in doing so, he had sealed his fate. He could never go back to her, never fix what had been broken.

There were times when he thought about the people he'd met on the road, the strangers who had crossed his path. They didn't know who he was, what he had done. To them, he was just another man, another face in the crowd, but he knew that every day was one day closer to the law catching up with him.

He passed through small towns where people stared at him, wondering who he was, but he never stayed long. He couldn't afford to, not with a price likely on his head. His only option now was to keep moving, to head south, to San Francisco, where the city's size would swallow him up, where he could disappear into the crowds and perhaps start over.

But even as he walked toward that distant city, he knew that starting over wasn't possible. Not for him. The past would always follow, would always be there, lurking in the corners of his mind, waiting for him to slip up.

One night, in a small town he was unfamiliar with, Gavin stood beside the tracks, watching a freight train rumble by. The sun had set, and the stars had started to twinkle, bright and cold in the vast, empty sky. He felt the familiar weight of the revolver at his hip, the cold steel that had become a constant companion since he'd killed Ellis. He knew the law was hunting him and could show up at any moment. He had to keep moving.

He thought about Shannon again, about the dreams they'd shared, and the love they'd had. She was gone, and nothing in this world could bring her back. He would never be able to make things right, never be able to fix the past.

Gavin climbed aboard the train as it slowed, jumping onto the flatbed car with practiced ease. He lay flat on his back, looking up at the stars as the train began to move again, carrying him south, toward San Francisco.

The train chugged along through the night, and Gavin closed his eyes, a deep, heavy sleep overtaking him. For the first time in a long while, he wasn't thinking about Ellis, or the law, or even the murder. He was thinking of Shannon—and he allowed himself the briefest of moments to mourn the life that had never come to pass.

***

The salty air of San Francisco hit Gavin's face like a slap as he stepped off the train, the bustling port city stretching out before him like a wild beast; its noise, smells, and hustle all jumbled into a cacophony of life. Ships from every corner of the world docked at the piers, their masts scraping the skies, their cargo spilling over the sides like an endless stream of goods. It was a city of promise, but also one of desperation—people came here in droves looking for fortune or a fresh start, only to find their dreams battered by the harsh reality of survival.

Gavin had no plans, no prospects. He was just a man running from his past, looking for a place to vanish. But a man without money and without skills couldn't make it very far. Not here. Not in San Francisco.

The bustling streets of San Francisco were a mishmash of sounds and activity, a sharp contrast to the quiet solitude of the mountains Gavin had left behind. The city teemed with life, but for a man with nothing but the clothes on his back and a few coins in his pocket, it was an unforgiving place.

Gavin walked the crowded avenues, his eyes scanning shop windows and bulletin boards for any sign of work. He asked at bakeries, stables, and even a blacksmith's forge, but the responses were all the same: "We're not hiring." The pity in their eyes stung almost as much as the rejection.

The days blurred together as he wandered the city, sleeping in alleyways or beneath the overhangs of buildings, his stomach aching with hunger. The cold nights bit at his skin, and the hard ground offered no comfort. Still, he refused to give up, driven by the same determination that had carried him this far.

One afternoon, as he sat on the edge of a fountain in the city square, staring at the water as it rippled in the sunlight, a man approached him. He was older, with a weathered face and a rough demeanor, his clothes stained from hard labor.

"You looking for work, son?" the man asked, his voice gruff but not unkind.

Gavin straightened, nodding. "I am. Can't seem to find any, though."

The man snorted. "That's 'cause you're lookin' in the wrong places. Folks in this city don't like to hire strangers. But if you're willin' to work hard, head down to the docks. They're always lookin' for laborers. Loading ships, hauling cargo—it's tough work, but it pays."

"The docks," Gavin repeated, a glimmer of hope flickering in his chest. "Thank you. I'll head there right away."

The man nodded, giving Gavin a pat on the shoulder. "Good luck to you. And keep your wits about you down there. Not everyone's friendly."

Gavin set off toward the waterfront, weaving through the throngs of people and carriages that crowded the streets. As he drew closer to the docks, the air grew heavy with the scent of salt and fish, and the cries of seagulls mingled with the shouts of sailors and stevedores.

The scene was chaotic: men hauling crates and barrels, ships creaking as they bobbed against the piers, and foremen barking orders over the din. It was a world of sweat and grit, but to Gavin, it was an opportunity.

He approached a group of men loading cargo onto a ship, his heart pounding with a mix of nerves and determination. "I'm looking for work," he said, addressing the foreman, a burly man named Finch.

Finch gave him a once-over, his sharp eyes taking in Gavin's lean frame and hardened expression. "You ever done dock work before?"

"No," Gavin admitted, "but I'm strong, and I learn fast."

The foreman grunted, motioning to a pile of crates. "Good enough. Start with those. Get 'em onto the deck. You do a decent job, I'll see about keeping you on."

Gavin nodded, rolling up his sleeves and getting

to work. The crates were heavy, the rough wood biting into his hands as he lifted them, but he didn't falter. Sweat poured down his face as he moved back and forth between the dock and the ship, his muscles straining with the effort.

By the end of the day, his body ached, and his hands were raw, Finch handed him a small handful of coins. It wasn't much, but it was more than he'd had in weeks.

"You did ok for a street rat," the foreman said. "Be here first thing tomorrow, and I'll put you on the roster. If you're a minute late, you're done."

Gavin nodded, a small smile tugging at his lips. It wasn't the life he had envisioned, but it was a start. For the first time in what felt like an eternity, he had a foothold—a chance to rebuild.

The job Gavin landed was as a laborer—hauling crates, barrels, and heavy bundles of goods from the ships onto the pier. The ships themselves were massive, towering above him like metal giants. The cargo was unloaded by men with thick, calloused hands, and their gruff voices mixed with the sound of chains creaking, pulleys groaning, and the rhythmic slap of wooden crates hitting the pier.

The work was relentless. From the first light of dawn until well after sunset, Gavin found himself lifting, carrying, and moving crates that seemed heavier than his own weight. They came in all shapes and sizes, from iron-bound boxes of machinery to delicate bundles of silk, and Gavin's hands were soon blistered and raw from the constant strain. The heat of the day was unbearable, the sun beating down with an intensity that made the salt air sting. And when the fog rolled in, it didn't bring any relief—just a thick, damp chill that soaked through his clothes and chilled his bones.

The men he worked alongside were mostly Irish immigrants, just like him. Some were older men who had seen too many years of hard work and hard living. Others were young and hopeful, like Gavin, but their eyes were dull with fatigue, their bodies bent from the constant toil. They spoke little, working in silence except for the occasional curse or shout when a crate slipped, or when tempers flared over lost time or spilled cargo. There was no time for anything else—no time for camaraderie, no time for kindness.

Lunch breaks were brief, if they came at all. The food was nothing more than stale bread and cheap meat, washed down with whatever whiskey or ale the men could afford. There were no comforts here—just work, sweat, and exhaustion. The docks were dangerous, too. Gavin had seen men fall from the rigging, their bodies crashing onto the hard wooden planks below, or worse, being crushed by the heavy cargo that sometimes slipped from the ropes. Accidents were common, but they were always quickly ignored—the work didn't stop, the goods didn't stop coming in.

The foreman was a cruel, hard man who cared only

about getting the work done. If you couldn't keep up, you were sent home without a second thought. If you complained, you were out on your ass, replaced by someone else who needed the job more. Gavin learned quickly that the docks weren't a place for weakness or hesitation. It was a place where you either kept your head down and worked, or you didn't survive.

And survive, he did. Day after day, Gavin's body grew stronger, his muscles hardening with the grueling labor. His hands toughened, and the sweat and exhaustion became a part of him. But it was also breaking him. The constant work, the long hours, the back pain, and the aching hunger—everything wore at him. There were moments when he'd catch himself looking out at the ships in the harbor, wondering if he'd ever escape the grind of the docks, wondering if there was any life left outside of this place. But those thoughts were fleeting—because the truth was, he didn't have a choice. The docks were his only option.

But amid the hard work, there were small moments of solidarity. The Irishmen who worked beside him didn't talk much, but they understood the grind. They'd nod to one another at the end of the day, silently acknowledging the shared struggle. Gavin learned a few words in Irish that he never knew before, little sayings that made the long hours bearable, like "Ar scáth a chéile a mhaireann na daoine"—people live in each other's shadows. It was a reminder that even in this hard, brutal place, they were all in it together, bound by the same struggles, the same desire for something better.

But even with that small sense of belonging, Gavin couldn't shake the feeling that he was still running—still trying to outrun the man he had been. Working on the docks, hauling crates under the warmth of the sun, it all felt like a temporary fix. It was enough to keep him alive, but it wasn't enough to stop the past from creeping in. At night, when he lay in the cramped, stinking boarding house with the sounds of the city swirling around him, he'd think about the life he'd left behind—about Shannon, about the baby, about the violence he had left in his wake. The past was never far, never quiet, and no matter how hard he worked, it always found a way to catch up.

The days blurred into each other at the docks, a haze of sweat and labor that seemed endless. Gavin's muscles were hardening, and his body was becoming accustomed to the constant strain, but so too was his temper. It was the relentless grind of the docks, the rough work, and the harsh treatment from Finch, that wore on him.

Finch was a bastard, a man who delighted in tormenting the workers. He was always scowling, barking orders, and taking every opportunity to belittle the men under his command. His voice was like the scraping of metal on stone, sharp and cutting. He had no patience for mistakes, no empathy for the weary, and no understanding of anything but getting the work done at any cost. He'd whip the workers into line with insults and threats, the kind of man who fed off the misery of others.

Gavin had learned early on to keep his head down, to follow orders without hesitation, because any sign of weakness was met with Finch's venom. But even Gavin, usually the quiet, brooding type, had limits.

It was late one afternoon, the sun dipping low behind the shipyards, when Finch picked his next target. The job had been hard that day, as it always was. Gavin's back ached from the constant lifting and hauling, his hands raw from the ropes and crates. He was barely keeping up with the pace, his body aching, and his mind tired. But that didn't matter to Finch.

"Move, Craite! Quit dawdling!" Finch barked, his voice like a whip cracking across Gavin's back.

Gavin's jaw clenched. The man had been on his case all day, finding fault in every move he made, criticizing the smallest mistakes, and calling him names like "lazy rat" or "useless scum." He had been patient at first, just trying to get through the workday without causing trouble, but something snapped inside him.

"I'm moving," Gavin said, his voice low but firm, his anger rising like a storm on the horizon.

Finch didn't care for Gavin's response. The foreman's eyes narrowed, and he took a step toward him, his voice dropping into a menacing growl. "You think you can talk back to me, boy? You think you're special? You're just another mule on my docks."

Gavin stood his ground. He didn't want trouble—he never did. But he was tired, tired of being treated like a dog, tired of the constant abuse. His fingers curled into fists as the anger in him boiled over.

"Quit your yapping, Finch. I'm doing my job," Gavin snapped, his tone sharp, his eyes flashing with a defiance he hadn't known he had left.

Finch stepped forward, towering over him, his face twisted with contempt. "I don't take backtalk from anyone. Not from you. Not from any of these bloody useless bastards."

He shoved Gavin hard, the impact knocking him back a few steps, sending a wave of pain through his spine. Gavin stumbled but caught his balance, his breath coming in heavy gasps. The men working nearby slowed their work, sensing the tension rising.

Gavin's temper flared. He couldn't take it anymore.

With a snarl, he swung at Finch, his fist connecting with the man's jaw. It wasn't a well-placed punch, but it was enough to knock Finch off-balance, sending him reeling. The foreman staggered, clutching his face in shock as the workers around them took a step back, watching in stunned silence.

"Don't ever touch me again," Gavin growled, his chest heaving.

But Finch wasn't about to back down. He recovered quickly, rage flashing in his eyes. Spitting blood, he lunged at Gavin, swinging wildly. The two men collided, fists flying, a blur of anger and frustration.

Gavin was faster, his youth and strength giving him an advantage, but Finch was a brawler, and his weight made him a difficult opponent. They grappled, each trying to land a solid punch, the sound of fists meeting flesh and the grunting of men filling the air.

For a moment, Gavin felt like he was going to win—like he could finally get out from under Finch's thumb. But then the foreman grabbed a nearby length of rope, swinging it at Gavin like a whip. The rope snapped against Gavin's side, the sting sharp and sudden, distracting him long enough for Finch to tackle him to the ground.

Gavin hit the dirt hard, the breath knocked out of him. Finch climbed on top, raining blows down on him, shouting obscenities, his rage a terrible force. Gavin fought back with everything he had, but it wasn't enough. The men around them had backed away, too afraid to interfere.

Finally, Finch stood, panting, and wiped the blood from his mouth. "You think you're tough, huh? You think you can just walk in here and cause trouble?" he spat.

Gavin struggled to his feet, wiping blood from his lip, his face bruised. He glared at Finch, but didn't speak. His body ached, his spirit crushed by the futility of it all.

"Get out of here, Craite. You're done," Finch sneered. "I don't need troublemakers on my docks."

Gavin stood there for a moment, staring at

the ground, his anger subsiding into a cold, bitter resignation. He didn't say a word. There was nothing left to say. Without a backward glance, he turned and walked away from the docks, the bitter taste of defeat lingering on his tongue.

The job had been a brief respite, a chance to disappear, but it had cost him more than he could afford. And now, once again, he was left with nothing but the open road and the memory of a past he couldn't escape.

CHAPTER 14

Gavin stumbled down the bustling streets of San Francisco, the ruthlessness of the city pressing in on him like a vice. His body ached from the beatings he'd endured—physical and emotional. He had no money, no food, and no place to call home. The docks had been a false hope, a fleeting moment of work that had ended in failure. The city was full of people just like him—lost, beaten down, struggling to stay afloat.

It was late afternoon, and the fog that rolled in from the bay clung to the streets, softening the harsh edges of the world. Gavin wandered the alleyways and corners, trying to stay out of sight of anyone who might recognize him. He'd been out here for days now, surviving on scraps and his wits, but it was becoming harder to keep his head above water.

As he passed a tavern, a group of rowdy sailors

spilled out onto the street, their laughter loud and unruly. Their eyes were glassy from too much drink, and they were looking for trouble, as men often did after too much time at sea. Gavin tried to slip by them, keeping his head down, but one of them noticed him—a stocky man with a thick, unkempt beard.

"Hey, young fella," the man slurred, a wide grin splitting his face. "You got a problem with us?"

Gavin didn't want trouble, but his stomach growled painfully, and he knew he needed to keep moving. He tried to ignore the man, walking faster, but the sailor's hand shot out, grabbing him by the arm.

"You hear me, boy?" the sailor spat, his breath reeking of alcohol. "I said, you got a problem?"

Gavin tensed, his hand inching toward his belt, where the dull handle of a knife was tucked in his coat. But before he could react, the sailor's friends had gathered around him, closing in like wolves circling a wounded deer.

"Leave me alone," Gavin muttered, trying to pull free.

But it was too late. The first blow came hard and fast, a punch to his gut that knocked the wind out of him. He stumbled, trying to regain his balance, but another sailor shoved him to the ground. Pain exploded across his ribs as he hit the hard cobblestone. The men laughed, kicking him in the side, taunting him in their drunken stupor.

"Stupid bastard," one of them sneered, delivering

another kick to his stomach.

Gavin gritted his teeth, trying to shield his face with his arms, but the beating was relentless. His vision blurred, and blood filled his mouth, but he wasn't going down without a fight. His fist lashed out, connecting with the knee of the sailor closest to him, but it wasn't enough. He was too weak, too outnumbered.

Just as one of the sailors reached down to grab him by the hair, a shout rang out from across the street.

"Oi! You lot, stop it!"

A tall man—broad-shouldered, with a sharp jaw and a coat that had seen better days—pushed his way through the group of sailors. His voice was calm, but there was an authority in it that made the sailors hesitate. They turned to see who was speaking.

"Back off, you drunken fools," the man said, his gaze sweeping over the group.

For a moment, the sailors wavered, unsure whether to pick a fight with the newcomer. But the man didn't back down. Instead, he stepped forward, his boots clicking on the cobblestones, and with a swift movement, he shoved one of the sailors away from Gavin.

"Leave him be, or I'll make you regret it," the man growled, his hands raised in a defensive stance.

The sailors, not wanting to escalate things further, muttered curses under their breath and backed off. They turned and staggered off down the street, leaving Gavin lying in the dirt, gasping for breath.

The man stood over him for a moment, watching them go, then knelt down beside Gavin. He had a quick look of concern on his face, but his demeanor was all business.

"Looks like you've had a rough day," the man said, offering a hand. "Get up."

Gavin reached for the man's hand, feeling the roughness of his skin and the firmness of his grip. He managed to push himself to his feet, but he was shaky, his ribs aching with every breath.

"Thanks," Gavin muttered, wiping the blood from his lip. "Didn't expect to find someone willing to step in."

The man gave a low chuckle, his eyes glinting with a hint of mischief. "Ain't the first time I've seen a bunch of drunks picking on someone smaller than them," he said. "You alright?"

Gavin nodded, though it was clear he was far from fine. His body was sore, his clothes torn, but he wasn't about to show weakness in front of this stranger.

"I'm good," Gavin said, trying to stand a little taller, but failing miserably.

The man eyed him for a moment, his expression unreadable. Then, he gave a slight nod.

"Name's Mike," he said. "You need a place to sleep tonight? You're gonna freeze out here if you don't find some shelter."

Gavin hesitated. He didn't trust easily, especially not after everything he had been through. But something in Mike's eyes—something that didn't look like the usual trickery—made him consider the offer.

"I don't have anywhere to go," Gavin admitted, his voice quiet. "Just... trying to survive."

Mike looked him over for a moment, then made a decision.

"Well, you can't do much surviving with a bunch of drunks beating the hell out of you every time you turn around," Mike said. "Come with me. I can get you sorted out. I know a place where you can rest, and I've got work for a man who's willing to put in the effort."

Gavin eyed him suspiciously. "What kind of work?"

Mike grinned, the hint of a wry smile tugging at the corners of his lips. "The kind that keeps your belly full and a roof over your head," he said. "No questions asked. But you'll owe me. And I don't take kindly to people who don't honor their debts."

Gavin weighed his options—what little options he had left. The street was no place for a man with nothing, and Mike seemed to know what he was talking about. With a sigh, Gavin nodded.

"Alright. I'll go with you."

Mike clapped him on the shoulder, his grip strong. "Good decision. Stick with me, and I'll show you how to stay alive in this city."

And just like that, Gavin's path was set. He didn't know it yet, but this meeting with Mike would change everything. The road ahead wouldn't be easy, but at least for now, he had someone who seemed to understand the rules of survival in a world that didn't care for the weak.

Mike "The Duke" Leduc had faced many men in his time, some fast and deadly, others slow and clumsy, but he knew that speed often mattered more than precision when it came to surviving in a world full of danger and deception. He could tell from the way Gavin carried himself that the boy had potential, but potential meant little unless it was honed. That's why, one cool evening as the orange glow of the setting sun stretched across the barren plains, Mike decided it was time to teach Gavin the most important lesson of all: how to shoot fast.

Mike took Gavin to a small creek on the edge of the city, a quiet spot far from prying eyes. The fire crackled softly as they ate their supper, but Mike's mind was already focused on the task ahead. After he finished chewing, he leaned back, giving Gavin a quick glance.

"Time to teach you something that might save your life," Mike said, his voice gravelly but calm.

Gavin looked at him, eyes narrowing in curiosity. "What's that?"

"The quick draw," Mike replied. "You ever seen a man pull his piece in the blink of an eye, shoot, and be back behind cover before you even knew what happened?"

Gavin shook his head. "I ain't never seen anyone that fast."

Mike smiled, an edge of mischief in his expression. "Well, that's because most folks pull their gun the wrong way. Watch me."

Mike stood up, moving gracefully for a man of his years, and pulled his pistol from its holster with a fluid motion. Instead of drawing it out and extending his arm like most men, he pushed his elbow back toward his body, the gun coming up in an arc to point straight ahead, all from the hip.

Gavin's eyes widened. The motion was fast, almost like magic. Mike grinned, knowing the boy would be impressed.

"See, most fools try to make their gun go out in front, arm extended, but that's too slow. You've gotta draw your pistol, and instead of pushing it out like you're some fancy sharpshooter, you pull it back to your hip. It's quicker, and once you get it down, it'll be like second nature."

Gavin furrowed his brow, still unsure. "But ain't it less accurate?"

Mike chuckled. "Yep, it's less accurate. But you don't need accuracy right away. You need speed. Accuracy comes with time. And once you practice enough, you won't even think about it anymore. It'll be as natural as breathing."

Mike set up a tin can on a rock some ten paces away, then turned back to Gavin.

"First thing's first. Get comfortable with your stance. Stand like you're ready for trouble, but relaxed. Don't stiffen up. Your gun's gotta feel like an extension of your body."

Gavin nodded and mimicked Mike's position, his body tense, but Mike could see the promise in him. He'd catch on quick, that much was certain.

"Now, follow me," Mike said, his voice low and commanding. "We're gonna do this slow at first. Pay attention to the movement. Elbow back, draw fast, and shoot without thinking."

Mike drew his gun, demonstrating the movement slowly, until Gavin could see the mechanics of it in his mind. Then, he took a deep breath.

"Alright, now your turn."

Gavin stepped forward and placed his hand on the handle of his revolver, fingers gripping it tight. He felt the heft of the steel in his palm and tried to match Mike's posture, unsure but determined.

"Now," Mike called, "let's see you do it."

Gavin pulled his gun awkwardly at first, the motion jerky and uncoordinated. The gun was almost too heavy for him, and the movement felt forced.

"No, no," Mike said, waving a hand. "Relax. You're too stiff. This ain't about muscle. It's about flow."

Mike stepped behind Gavin and placed a hand on his arm, gently guiding him. "Feel the motion. Your elbow's gotta pull back, and your gun's gotta follow, no pushing it out like you're throwing a punch. It's a fluid motion. Let your body do the work."

Gavin nodded, sweat starting to form on his brow as he tried again. The second attempt was smoother, but still not fast enough. Mike watched him closely, nodding with approval at the improvement, even if it was slight.

"Not bad," Mike said, "but we ain't done yet. Keep practicing. It's all about repetition, getting it in your blood. When you're quick enough, you'll surprise a man before he even knows you've got your gun out."

Over the next few hours, the two of them worked under the fading light. Mike barked out commands, coaching Gavin, reminding him to keep his movements loose and natural. It was frustrating for Gavin, the motion still clumsy, but he knew he had to push through.

By the time the stars started to twinkle above, Gavin's hand was aching, and his mind was focused on nothing but that damned motion—elbow back, draw, aim, shoot. Over and over.

Mike didn't let up, and slowly, Gavin's movements became faster, more fluid, until the gunshot from his revolver echoed in the still night air in near perfect timing with the draw. His speed had increased, though the accuracy was still lacking.

Mike smiled, watching the boy with approval. "There you go. You're getting the hang of it."

Gavin stood there, breathing heavy, a tired grin on his face. "Feels like it's gonna take a lot of practice."

"It will," Mike agreed. "But you're on the right track, kid. Keep at it, and one day, you won't even think about it. It'll just happen."

Mike gave him a hard slap on the back. "Tomorrow, we start again. And this time, we make it even quicker."

Gavin nodded, eyes glinting with determination. "I'll be ready."

Mike just laughed, the sound deep and full of experience. "That's what I like to hear."

The night settled in around them, but for Gavin, the practice had already begun to sink in. The next time he drew his gun, it might just be fast enough to save his life.

CHAPTER 15

Gavin leaned against the worn railing of the cramped room he and Mike called home, the faint smell of salt air wafting in through the open window. Mike was pacing the floor, his boots thudding softly on the wooden planks, his hands gesturing as he spoke.

"Listen, Gavin," Mike said, his voice low and persuasive. "You've seen how hard it is out there. The docks break men, the streets chew them up. But there's a better way—a smarter way."

Gavin crossed his arms, frowning. "A smarter way that involves robbing banks? You're talking about stealing, Mike. I didn't come to this city to become a common criminal."

Mike stopped pacing and turned to face him, a grin spreading across his face. "Stealing? You think I'm talking about picking pockets or knocking over saloons? No, my friend. This isn't about petty theft.

This is about justice."

"Justice?" Gavin scoffed, raising an eyebrow. "Since when does holding up a bank count as justice?"

Mike leaned in, his voice dropping to a conspiratorial whisper. "Because it's not about the money, not really. It's about who we're taking it from. Think about it, Gavin—the banks aren't run by your average Joe. They're run by the government, the same government that taxes a man into poverty and leaves him to rot in the streets. The same government that sends its enforcers to crush anyone who dares to stand up for themselves."

Gavin hesitated, the words sinking in. Mike had a way of making things sound… righteous. Like the law wasn't black and white but shades of gray.

"You really believe that?" Gavin asked, his voice softer now.

Mike nodded; his eyes gleaming. "I do. And I'll prove it to you. I've got a plan—something clean, something smart. No blood, no unnecessary risks. We hit a bank, take what we need, and move on. Simple as that."

"And what's my part in all this?" Gavin asked, his arms still crossed but his resolve beginning to waver.

"You, my friend, are the perfect inside man," Mike said, a sly smile curling his lips. "Clean up, put on some nice clothes, and stroll into the bank like you belong there. Open an account, chat up the tellers, and get a feel for the place. Security, vault placement, staff routines—the whole layout."

Gavin frowned. "And then what? You just walk in and start waving a gun around?"

Mike chuckled. "Not quite. Here's the beauty of it. When we go back a few days later, I'll be the one holding up the place. But to everyone inside, you'll be just another poor soul caught up in the chaos. I'll make it look like I'm forcing you to help me. You fill the bag, I take you 'hostage,' and we ride out of town. By the time they put the pieces together, we'll be long gone."

Gavin rubbed the back of his neck, conflicted. The plan was audacious, almost absurdly so. But Mike's confidence was infectious, and the idea of striking back at the powers that had beaten him down all his life was tempting. Still, a part of him hesitated.

"I don't know, Mike. What if something goes wrong?"

Mike clapped him on the shoulder, his grin widening. "That's the thing, Gavin. We plan it out, we control the risks. I've done this before. Trust me, you'll be safe."

Gavin sighed, his resistance crumbling. Mike had a way of making you believe in him, even when you knew better. "Alright," he said finally. "I'll do it. But if this goes south—"

"Gavin, like I said. It won't," Mike interrupted, his tone confident. "You'll see, Gavin. This is the start of something big. Stick with me, and we'll rewrite the rules."

Over the next few days, Mike and Gavin made their preparations, scoping out various banks in the small towns surrounding them. Gavin learned quickly, observing everything from the positioning of security guards to the layout of the cash registers. With each outing, his confidence grew, and Mike's infectious spirit became a guiding light, pulling him from the shadows of his past.

A week later, Gavin tugged at the collar of his borrowed jacket, the fabric stiff against his neck. He stepped into the bank, the smell of ink and money heavy in the air. The room was polished and orderly, the tellers busy with customers, and a uniformed guard stood near the door. He forced himself to smile, nodding politely as he approached the counter.

"Good afternoon," he said, his voice steady. "I'd like to open an account."

The teller, a middle-aged man with a thin mustache, smiled back. "Of course, sir. If you'll just fill out this form."

As Gavin scribbled on the paper, he let his eyes wander, taking in every detail—the placement of the guard, the swinging door leading to the back offices, and the heavy steel vault nestled behind a desk. He asked casual questions, laughed at the teller's small talk, and made a mental map of everything he saw.

When he left the bank an hour later, he knew the layout like the back of his hand. He found Mike waiting for him in a nearby alley, leaning against a wall with his hat pulled low.

"Well?" Mike asked, his tone eager.

Gavin nodded. "It's all there. Guard's not too sharp, vault's in the back. Shouldn't be too hard to pull off."

Mike grinned, clapping him on the back. "That's the spirit, lad. Now let's get to work. Tomorrow, we make history."

Gavin nodded, his heart racing at the idea. The adrenaline coursed through him, a welcome distraction from his grief. "And what if they catch me?"

"They won't," Mike said confidently. "You'll be fine. Just act natural. If you play your part right, you'll be a customer caught in the crossfire. They'll give us what we want to keep things calm."

Finally, the day arrived. Gavin felt a mix of anticipation and dread as they stood outside the chosen bank, the early morning sun casting a golden glow over the building. Mike adjusted his hat, the excitement radiating off him like heat from a flame. "Ready, Gavin?"

Gavin took a deep breath, squaring his shoulders. "As ready as I'll ever be."

"Perfect! Remember, just keep your cool. We'll get what we need, and then we'll be out in a flash." With that, Mike flashed a cheeky smile and motioned for Gavin to enter the bank.

Gavin's heart was pounding in his chest. The bank

was bustling with customers and clerks, the air thick with the scent of ink and paper. He made his way to a teller, casually glancing around while trying to appear nonchalant. He exchanged a few words with the teller, a friendly woman with kind eyes, and quickly scanned the layout, noting the exits.

Moments later, Mike burst into the bank, a gun drawn and a wild look in his eyes. "Everyone down!" he shouted, his voice booming through the space.

Gavin's heart dropped as chaos erupted around them. People screamed, scrambling to get low, while Gavin stood frozen for a moment. He hadn't expected the sheer intensity of the moment, the adrenaline surging through him like electricity. Mike spotted him and waved him forward.

Pointing at Gavin, Mike barked "You! Get over here!"

Gavin rushed to Mike's side, his instincts kicking in, he whispered. "You said to act natural!"

"Natural, yes, but we're in a bit of a situation now!" Mike shot back, a grin spreading across his face as he turned back to the crowd. "Everyone listen up! This is a simple job. Just do as I say, and nobody gets hurt!"

Mike turned his attention to the tellers, waving his gun. "You, get the cash! Now!"

Gavin watched in awe as Mike commanded the room with an effortless charm, the chaos morphing into a wild dance. The tellers scrambled to gather money, and Gavin felt the thrill of it all coursing through him.

It was reckless, dangerous, and intoxicating.

As the teller filled the bag with cash, Mike pointed his gun at Gavin and ordered him to pick it up. "You grab that bag." Mike's eyes were sparkling with mischief.

Moments later, the bag was full, and Mike kept his gun on Gavin. "Y'all count to 200 hundred before anyone gets up. If I see anyone one of y'as coming out before then, I'm a shoot this man right in the head."

Mike gave Gavin a nudge. "Please just do what he says" Gavin pleaded as convincingly as he could.

Together, they sprinted out of the bank, the sound of footsteps and shouts following them. Gavin's pulse pounded in his ears as they raced down the street, adrenaline driving them forward. They reached their horses tied to a post, and Gavin hopped on, his heart racing with exhilaration.

As Mike mounted his own horse, he turned to Gavin, laughter bubbling up from his throat. "See? Easy as pie!"

Gavin couldn't help but join in, the thrill of the heist lifting his spirits for the first time in months. They rode hard, escaping the chaos behind them, the sound of hooves echoing against the cobblestones as they left the bank—and the town—behind.

"Where to next?" Gavin asked, his chest heaving with exhilaration.

Mike grinned, the wind whipping through his hair. "Anywhere we damn well please! Welcome to the life of a bank robber, my friend!"

As they rode off into the horizon, Gavin felt a spark of hope igniting within him. He was no longer a man burdened by his past; he was Gavin Craite, a partner in crime, and for the first time in a long while, he felt alive.

CHAPTER 16

Life had a way of surprising Gavin, twisting him through the currents of fate with a ruthless elegance. After months of pulling off heists with Mike, Gavin found himself living a life he never imagined possible. They had become legends in their own right, notorious for their audacious bank robberies that left the townsfolk buzzing with excitement and fear. Each successful job brought not only a bounty of cash but also a thrill that coursed through Gavin's veins like fire.

Mike was the life of the party, spinning tales of their exploits and filling the air with laughter and camaraderie. They would ride into a town, often dressed as ordinary cowboys, only to vanish moments later with bags full of stolen cash. They celebrated their victories in seedy saloons, drowning in whiskey and stories, the world at their fingertips.

One evening, they found themselves seated at a rickety table in a dimly lit tavern in a small town just outside the border. The air was thick with the smell of tobacco and spilled drinks, and laughter rang out from the corners as patrons reveled in the freedom of the night. Mike was animated, recounting their latest robbery with all the flair of a seasoned performer.

"Did you see the look on that teller's face when I pulled out my piece? She thought it was a damn joke!" Mike laughed, slapping the table.

Gavin chuckled; the memories of their latest escapade still fresh in his mind. They had hit a small bank in a neighboring town, and their timing had been impeccable. "And how about that one guard who tried to play the hero? I thought he was going to faint when he saw you!"

The laughter echoed, and Gavin felt a warmth wash over him. It was a brief reprieve from the haunting memories that had once consumed him. For the first time since he'd fled his past, he felt a sense of belonging, a camaraderie that dulled the edges of his pain.

However, the high life came with its own set of dangers, a truth they both knew but chose to ignore. Word of their escapades had spread like wildfire, and soon, a marshal had caught wind of their trail. Marshal Vincent Boone was known for his tenacity, his reputation built on bringing down outlaws, and Gavin could sense the shift in the air. It wasn't long before Boone set his sights on them.

***

The sheriff's office was dimly lit by a pair of kerosene lamps, their soft glow illuminating the faces of Sheriff Boone and his deputies, Virgil and Otis. A large, weathered map of the territory was spread across the desk, corners held down by tin cups and a stack of wanted posters. Sheriff Boone, a grizzled man with a thick mustache and a steely gaze, leaned over the map, his finger tracing a path between towns.

"They've been smart about it," Boone began, his voice a low rumble, "but not smart enough. Look here." He tapped three red circles he'd drawn on the map. "Pecos, Dry Gulch, and Clearwater. Each hit a week apart, always on a Friday. Midday."

Virgil, the younger of the two deputies, scratched his head. "So, they like Fridays? What's that tell us?"

Boone shot him a look that could've split wood. "It tells us they're methodical. These lowlifes are sticking to a pattern, whether they realize it or not. That gives us something to work with."

Otis, older and wiry with a permanent scowl, leaned closer, squinting at the map. "What's their route?"

"They're moving in a rough circle," Boone said, dragging his finger from the most recent robbery in Clearwater to the next likely targets. "They're not backtracking, so we can rule out the places they've already hit. But they're heading into smaller towns now—less security, bigger payoff for them. They've got at least three options ahead: Willow Creek, Lonesome Ridge, and Silver Bend."

Virgil frowned. "You think they'd hit all three?"

"Not likely. They'll pick one. But we're gonna be ready for 'em, no matter which they choose."

Boone stepped back from the desk, crossing his arms as he addressed his deputies. "We'll set traps at all three. Otis, you'll take Willow Creek. Virgil, you'll cover Lonesome Ridge. I'll head to Silver Bend. Now, listen close, because this plan's gotta be tight."

He pointed to each town on the map. "Otis, Willow Creek's bank is small, only got two clerks and one guard. Hide your men in the hardware store across the street. When the boys roll in, they'll come in fast and loud. You let them get inside before you spring the trap. Block their way out."

Otis nodded, his mouth twitching into a grim line. "Understood."

"Virgil, Lonesome Ridge is trickier. The bank sits on the edge of town, near open fields. They'll use that to escape if we're not careful. Station a man on the roof of the saloon and another in the livery. Pin 'em in from both sides."

Virgil adjusted his hat, looking nervous. "What if they bolt before we can close in?"

Boone fixed him with a hard stare. "Then you make damn sure your men have good aim."

He moved his finger to Silver Bend, where the largest bank in the region stood. "This is where I'll be. Silver Bend's bank has iron bars on the windows, so they'll have to come through the front door. I'll place two men in the telegraph office next door and another pair disguised as customers inside the bank. The minute they step through that door, we'll surround 'em."

Virgil shifted uneasily. "What if they come gunning? These boys ain't afraid to shoot."

Boone's jaw tightened. "That's why we take the first shot if we have to. I'd rather bring them in alive, but I won't risk losing a deputy to these outlaws. If they draw, we end it."

The room fell silent for a moment, the gravity of Boone's words settling over them. Finally, Otis broke the silence. "You think they'll fall for it?"

"Ain't nothing to fall for. They're just gonna keep on doing what they've been doing. But this time it'll be different. Cause we'll be waiting," Boone said. If we play this right, their luck runs out by this Friday or the next."

Boone rolled up the map and handed it to Otis. "Spread the word to the other deputies and local sheriffs. No one moves alone, and everyone keeps their eyes peeled. Let's put an end to this."

The deputies nodded, determination replacing their doubts. As they filed out, Boone stood by the window, watching the darkened street.

***

The Willow Creek Bank was modest—a single-story building with a painted wooden sign swinging gently in the breeze. Gavin sat on a bench inside, his hat resting on his knee as he waited for the teller to finish updating the ledger. He played the part of a polite ranch hand, offering a sheepish grin when the old man behind the counter commented on the weather.

"Warm spell's holdin' out longer than usual," the teller remarked, his voice gravelly with age.

"Sure is," Gavin replied, his tone easy, his gaze darting around the room. He took in every detail: the narrow layout, the iron-barred windows, and the heavy oak door leading to the vault in the back. A single guard leaned against the far wall, more interested in his pocket watch than his surroundings.

The teller handed Gavin a receipt for his deposit—ten dollars he was planning on "withdrawing" the following day. "There you go, Mr. Hayes," the man said, offering a kind smile.

"Thank you, sir," Gavin replied, tipping his hat as he stood.

He lingered for a moment by the door, pretending to adjust his boot while he noted the position of the safe and the stack of ledgers behind the counter. He glanced through the front window, tracing the path to the alley he'd seen earlier. Satisfied, he stepped outside, the bell above the door jingling faintly as it closed behind him.

Later that evening, Gavin returned to the small campsite he shared with Mike, just beyond the tree line outside of town. The fire crackled low, casting flickering light on Mike's rugged face as he leaned back against a log, sharpening his knife.

"Well?" Mike asked without looking up.

Gavin tossed his hat onto the ground and sat down, running a hand through his hair. "It's as simple as they come. Two tellers, one guard. Vault's in the back. No more than a five-minute job."

Mike grinned, his teeth catching the firelight. "And the layout?"

"Front entrance opens straight to the counter. Iron bars on the windows, so that's out. Best bet's the alley behind the bakery. We can stash the horses there. Quiet getaway."

Mike nodded, considering the plan as he tested the blade against his thumb. "The safe. You get a good look?"

Gavin shook his head. "Didn't want to push my luck. It's a small one, though. Same as the one in Dry Gulch."

"Which means a simple lock," Mike said, his grin widening.

"Exactly."

Mike set the knife down and leaned forward, his sharp eyes locking onto Gavin's. "Alright. Here's what we do. We hit 'em Friday, midday. Town'll be busy enough that no one notices us strollin' in, but not so busy we can't control the crowd. You go in ahead to make your withdrawal as per usual. He'll have to open the safe then I'll come in and do all the fun stuff. I'll handle the guard and the tellers; you clean out the safe."

"And the horses?" Gavin asked.

"We tie 'em behind the bakery," Mike said, gesturing toward the town with his chin. "It's close enough to the alley for a quick escape. Once we're clear of the alley, we cut west to the ridge. They'll expect us to head south, so we double back once we're out of sight."

Gavin nodded, his expression thoughtful. "What if someone walks in on us? Bank's in the middle of town."

Mike's grin faded, replaced by a hard edge. "Then we remind 'em why they shouldn't. Quick and clean. No hesitation."

"Maybe we oughtta quit while we're winning the game? Eventually it's gonna catch up to us." Gavin suggested.

Mike, ever the optimist, waved off Gavin's concerns. "Pfft! We've outsmarted the best of them. Let em try. We'll just pull another job and leave 'em in the dust."

As Gavin closed his eyes that night he couldn't shake the feeling of impending doom. The thrill of the chase had turned into a dangerous game, one that left Gavin feeling more like prey than predator.

The late morning sun poured over Willow Creek, casting a golden glow on its quiet streets. After a hearty breakfast at their hotel, Gavin adjusted his hat and headed to the bank. As he stepped up onto the wooden porch of the bank, the familiar creak of the planks beneath his boots did little to ease the tension twisting in his gut. He'd been in and out of this bank twice already that week, but today felt different.

The town was quieter than usual, the occasional murmur of townsfolk carrying in the breeze. Gavin opened the door, the small bell above jingling softly as he stepped inside.

It was empty.

Other than the teller, who wasn't the old man Gavin had spoken to before. This one was younger, leaner, with sharp eyes that tracked Gavin the moment he entered.

Gavin hesitated, his instincts prickling. Something was off.

"Morning," the new teller said, his voice steady but with an edge Gavin didn't like.

"Morning," Gavin replied, tipping his hat. He approached the counter slowly, his boots echoing in the quiet space.

The room felt smaller than it had before, the air thick with an unease Gavin couldn't shake. His gaze flicked to the corner where the guard usually stood. The spot was empty.

"That's odd," Gavin thought, his stomach

tightening.

He opened his mouth to make polite small talk, but the words didn't come. Something told him to leave, to get out while he still could. He turned slightly toward the door—

And then it burst open.

Mike stormed in, his revolver drawn and his face lit with a wild grin. "Hands in the air!" he bellowed.

It happened in an instant. The new teller's calm demeanor vanished, replaced by a sharp, calculated movement as he pulled a gun from beneath the counter.

The crack of the shot echoed through the bank like a thunderclap.

Mike staggered back, clutching his side as blood seeped through his shirt. "Damn it!" he roared, firing wildly in the teller's direction.

Gavin dove for cover behind a desk, his heart pounding as the chaos erupted. Splinters flew as bullets tore through the wood around him. He scrambled to draw his own gun but hesitated—he knew they were in the wrong and couldn't justify firing at the teller.

"Gavin!" Mike yelled, his voice ragged with pain. "Move!"

Gavin's instincts kicked in. He darted toward the side door, staying low as the teller fired again, the shot grazing his hat and sending it spinning to the floor.

"Damn it, Mike!" Gavin shouted as he reached the door. "This was a setup!"

Mike didn't respond, too focused on returning

fire as he stumbled toward the exit. Gavin grabbed his arm, dragging him through the door into the back alley.

They dashed for the side exit, but chaos reigned as gunshots rang out, the noise deafening in Gavin's ears. He and Mike sprinted down the narrow alley, adrenaline propelling them forward. But as they reached the end, Deputy Marshal Otis Bates, along with the local sheriff and his deputies, emerged from the shadows, blocking their path.

"Mike! Go!" Gavin shouted, pushing his friend forward as he turned to confront their pursuers.

In the split second of confusion, Gavin felt the weight of despair settle over him. Mike, never one to back down, turned and faced the deputies, his bravado shining through the fear. "I'm not going down without a fight!"

"No! Mike, don't!" Gavin yelled, but it was too late. Mike reloaded his gun and began firing shots at the approaching officers. The sound of gunfire rang out, and Gavin's heart sank as he watched the scene unfold in slow motion.

Amid the chaos, a single shot echoed above the others, a sickening thud cutting through the cacophony. Gavin's breath caught in his throat as he saw Mike stagger backward, a second hit brought blood blooming across his shirt. Time froze as he rushed to his friend's side, cradling Mike's head in his arms as life faded from his eyes.

"Mike! No!" Gavin cried, the sense of loss crashing down on him like a tidal wave.

"I… I'm fine," Mike gasped, his voice strained. "Just… get outta here, Gavin. You have to run."

Tears blurred Gavin's vision as he shook his head. "I can't leave you!"

"Go! They'll take you down, too!" Mike urged, his voice growing weaker. "Promise me, Gavin. You have to survive. You have to—"

Before Gavin could respond, Mike's eyes met his, the life draining from his body. A howl of grief tore from Gavin's throat, a sound that echoed his soul's despair. The chaos of the bank faded into the background as Gavin's world collapsed around him.

The sheriff's deputies closed in; their guns trained on Gavin. With his last ounce of strength and spirit, Mike began firing in the direction of the lawmen, distracting their focus and giving Gavin the opening he needed to escape. He had to move. He couldn't let Mike's sacrifice be in vain. With a final, anguished look at his fallen friend, Gavin tore himself away and sprinted down the alley, his heart pounding as he fought through the pain.

As the gunfire erupted behind him, Gavin felt a surge of desperation. He could hear the shouts of the deputies, the sounds of pursuit echoing through the streets. He raced through the winding alleys, his mind racing with thoughts of escape. He had no plan, only the instinct to survive. He found his and Mike's horses, mounting up as his lungs burned gasping for air.

As he rode out of town, he heard the gun fire slow down and then cease. He knew he was alone again. He pushed himself forward, the air heavy with smoke and the scent of gunpowder. He rode into another alley, narrowly avoiding a group of townsfolk who stood frozen in shock. He had to get away; he had to find a place to hide.

After what felt like an eternity, he finally found refuge in the dense woods bordering the town. He wasn't followed. Breathless and shaking, he stumbled through the underbrush, his heart pounding in his chest. Gavin dismounted, sank to the ground, laying against a tree as he tried to catch his breath. Mike was gone. Grief burrowed deeply into his soul, suffocating and relentless. Gavin pressed his forehead against the rough bark, tears streaming down his face as he mourned the loss of his friend and the life he had embraced.

He had escaped, but at what cost? In that moment, Gavin realized that the thrill of the high life was a fleeting illusion, one that came with devastating consequences. The path he had chosen was now fraught with danger, and he was once again a man on the run, haunted by the ghosts of his past and the burden of his choices.

As the sun dipped below the horizon, Gavin knew he had to keep moving. He could not allow

Mike's sacrifice to be in vain. But where could he go? The world stretched out before him, a vast expanse of uncertainty and fear. Yet deep within, a flicker of determination ignited. He would survive. He would find a way to honor Mike's memory.

And so, Gavin Craite, once a simple cattle farmer's son, again became a fugitive, racing into the darkness with the sins of his past clinging to him like a shadow.

CHAPTER 17

Gavin sat hunched over the bar, the rim of his glass pressed to his lips as he stared blankly into the amber liquid within. The saloon buzzed around him, full of laughter, clinking glasses, and the faint strains of a piano in the corner. But to him, it was just noise, muffled and distant, like the world was happening far away from where he sat.

He was drunk, though not enough to forget. Mike's face lingered in his mind, pale and still in the aftermath of the robbery gone wrong. His only friend was gone, and the weight of that loss bore down on him like a millstone. He tipped the glass back, swallowing the last of the whiskey, and signaled for another.

"Rough night?" a voice broke through the fog of his thoughts.

Gavin glanced up, his bleary eyes meeting those of a woman leaning against the bar. Her sharp blue eyes held a mixture of curiosity and something softer, almost like concern. She was striking, with auburn hair swept into loose curls and a confidence that seemed out of place in the dim, smoky saloon.

"More like a rough life," he muttered, his voice hoarse.

She chuckled, a low, melodic sound. "Well, you're in the right place for that." She nodded toward the bartender, who slid another glass his way. Without asking, she ordered a drink for herself and took the stool next to him.

"Name's Rebecca," she said, extending a hand.

Gavin hesitated, then shook it briefly. "Gavin."

"Gavin," she repeated, letting the name roll off her tongue. "Irish?"

"Parents were. But I was born on this side of the world," he replied, taking another sip.

Rebecca studied him for a moment, her gaze sharp and discerning. "You look like a man carrying more than just whiskey in that glass."

Gavin gave a bitter laugh. "You could say that."

"Want to talk about it?" she asked, tilting her head slightly.

"Not much to say," he replied, setting the glass down harder than he intended. "Lost my only friend. He gave me a new life, and now he's gone."

Rebecca's expression softened, and for a moment, neither of them spoke. The noise of the saloon faded into the background, leaving just the two of them at the bar. Finally, she reached out and placed a hand over his.

"I'm sorry," she said quietly. "Losing someone like that... it's not something you get over. But drowning yourself in whiskey won't bring him back."

Gavin looked at her, startled by the sincerity in her voice. He opened his mouth to respond, but the words caught in his throat. Instead, he nodded, a small, reluctant gesture of acknowledgment.

Rebecca stood and extended her hand again, this time in invitation. "Come on. You look like you could use some company."

Gavin hesitated, glancing at the glass in his hand. He'd come to the saloon to be alone, to lose himself in the haze of alcohol and forget the world outside. But something about Rebecca's presence, her warmth and steadiness, drew him in. He set the glass down and took her hand.

She led him upstairs, the creak of the wooden stairs loud in the quiet hallway above the saloon. Her room was modest, with a small bed, a washbasin, and a single oil lamp casting a soft glow. She closed the door behind them and turned to face him.

"Sit," she said, motioning to the edge of the bed.

Gavin obeyed, feeling unsteady on his feet. Rebecca moved closer, her hands brushing his shoulders as she leaned in. Her touch was gentle, but there was an undeniable purpose in her movements.

"You've been carrying this burden for too long,"

she murmured. "Let me help you forget, just for a little while."

He didn't resist as she leaned in, her lips finding his in a kiss that was both tender and insistent. Her hands slid down his arms, guiding him back onto the bed. For the first time in what felt like forever, Gavin allowed himself to let go, to lose himself in the solace Rebecca offered.

Later, as they lay tangled in the sheets, Rebecca traced lazy circles on his chest. "You're not as alone as you think," she said softly. "Sometimes it just takes the right person to remind you."

Gavin didn't respond, his thoughts too muddled to form words. But as sleep claimed him, he held onto the faint glimmer of comfort she'd given him, a tiny ember in the darkness of his grief.

The morning sunlight streamed through the thin curtains, casting a warm glow across the modest room. Gavin stirred, blinking groggily as he adjusted to the light. For a moment, he didn't know where he was, the events of the night before blurred by whiskey and exhaustion. Then he felt the warmth of another body beside him.

Rebecca was already awake, propped up on one elbow and watching him with a small, knowing smile. "Good morning," she said, her voice soft but steady.

Gavin groaned, running a hand through his tousled hair. "Morning," he muttered, his voice rough with sleep.

She handed him a glass of water from the nightstand. "Drink. You'll thank me later."

He accepted it without protest, draining the glass in a few gulps. Setting it aside, he looked at her, taking in the unguarded warmth in her eyes. For the first time in weeks, he felt something other than the gnawing ache of loss—a flicker of connection.

"You didn't have to stay," he said quietly.

Rebecca shrugged. "Didn't have to, but I wanted to. You looked like you needed someone."

He nodded, the weight of her words settling over him. Reaching into the pocket of his coat draped over a chair, he pulled out a wad of cash and handed it to her. "Here. Consider this... a retainer. I don't want to be alone."

Rebecca took the money, her brows lifting in surprise, but she didn't refuse. Instead, she tucked it into her dress and looked back at him. "All right. But if you're going to stick around, you're coming with me. There's more to life than this room and that saloon."

Gavin frowned. "What do you mean?"

"You'll see," she said with a small smile. "Get dressed. We're going to my house."

An hour later, they arrived at a modest cottage on the outskirts of town. Rebecca pushed open the door and ushered him inside. The scent of baking bread greeted them, and a small boy of about six or seven ran to Rebecca, wrapping his arms around her legs.

"This is Joseph," she said, scooping the boy up and

kissing his cheek. "My son."

Gavin's eyes widened slightly, but he said nothing, merely nodding in acknowledgment. A woman appeared from the kitchen, wiping her hands on an apron. She was a few years older than Rebecca, with the same auburn hair but a sterner demeanor.

"And this is my sister, Maude," Rebecca continued. "She's a schoolteacher and helps me take care of Joseph."

Maude gave Gavin a critical once-over but said nothing, simply nodding in greeting. Gavin felt out of place in the cozy, bustling home, but there was a strange comfort in its warmth and simplicity.

Rebecca set Joseph down and turned to Gavin. "This is my world," she said, gesturing around the room. "It's not much, but it's mine. And if you're going to stick around, you can be part of it as long as you can afford to, but I'll warn you now. You step outta line even an inch, you're gone. No second chances either, you mess up and I'll put one in ya. Rebecca pulled out a small pistol she kept in her dress. But I'm sure it won't come to that, right sweety?"

Gavin smiled "Deal."

CHAPTER 18

For the first time in a long while, Gavin felt a glimmer of hope—a faint but persistent sense that maybe, just maybe, he could find a place in the world again

Gavin adjusted quickly to life in Rebecca's home. The cottage was small but lively, filled with the laughter of Joseph and the steady rhythm of Maude's work in the kitchen or at her desk grading papers. To his surprise, Gavin found himself gravitating toward the boy. At first, Joseph was shy, peeking around corners to watch him with wide, curious eyes. But soon enough, the little boy was tugging at his hand, eager for attention.

"You wanna go fishing?" Joseph asked one morning, his brown eyes sparkling with excitement.

Gavin hesitated but nodded. "Sure, kid. Go grab your boots."

He spent the day teaching Joseph how to bait a hook and cast a line. They sat side by side on the riverbank, the boy chattering endlessly while Gavin listened with a faint smile. When Joseph caught his first fish—a small perch—his shrieks of joy echoed through the trees.

"You're a natural," Gavin said, ruffling the boy's hair.

That evening, Gavin showed Joseph how to hold his fists up properly. "If someone tries to hurt you or your mama, you fight back," he said. "But only when you have to. Understand?"

Joseph nodded solemnly, mimicking Gavin's stance. "Like this?"

"That's it," Gavin said with a grin. "Now, throw a punch."

Later, he took the boy to the edge of the field behind the house and set up empty cans on a fence post. Rebecca watched from the porch as Gavin showed Joseph how to handle a small rifle.

"Take your time," Gavin instructed. "Breathe. Focus on the can, not the gun."

Rebecca frowned slightly but said nothing, her arms crossed as she observed them. When Joseph hit his first target, he let out a triumphant yell, and Gavin clapped him on the shoulder.

"You'll make a fine marksman someday," he said.

That night, as Joseph slept, Rebecca approached Gavin in the dim light of the sitting room. "He's just a boy," she said softly. "You're teaching him things… dangerous things."

"I'm teaching him how to survive," Gavin replied, his voice low. "This world isn't kind, Rebecca. He needs to be ready."

Rebecca sighed but didn't argue. She touched his arm gently. "Thank you for spending time with him. It means a lot."

Gavin nodded, the unspoken understanding between them settling like a fragile truce.

A few days later, the peace Gavin had found began to crumble. As he chopped wood behind the house, a memory struck him—a flash of the chaotic gunfire that had ended Mike's life. He could still hear the shouts, the pounding of his heart, and the sickening thud of his friend hitting the ground.

His hands trembled, and the axe slipped from his grip, embedding itself in the stump with a loud thwack. Gavin staggered back, his breath coming in shallow gasps. The heartache from the memory pressed down on him, suffocating.

Without a word, he left the yard and headed to the saloon.

Gavin slammed his glass down on the bar, the burn of whiskey doing little to dull the edge of his anguish. Around him, the saloon buzzed with activity, but he was deaf to it all. His focus was on the storm raging inside him.

A man bumped into him, spilling his drink.

"Watch it," the stranger snarled.

Gavin turned slowly, his eyes cold and unyielding. "You got a problem?"

The man sneered. "Yeah, I do. You're in my seat."

What followed was a blur of fists and broken chairs. Gavin fought like a man possessed, his rage unchecked. It wasn't until a familiar voice cut through the chaos that he paused.

"Gavin!" Rebecca's voice was sharp, commanding.

She stood in the entrance of the saloon, her eyes blazing. The room fell silent as she marched forward, grabbing his arm and dragging him outside.

"What the hell are you doing?" she demanded once they were in the street.

Gavin swayed slightly, wiping blood from his lip. "Needed to blow off some steam."

Rebecca's jaw tightened, her expression a mix of anger and concern. "You can't keep doing this, Gavin. You're going to get yourself killed."

"Maybe that's what I deserve," he muttered, avoiding her gaze.

Rebecca stepped closer, her voice softening. "Mike wouldn't want this for you. And neither do I."

Her words hit him like a punch to the gut. He looked at her, the fight draining out of him. "I don't know how to stop," he admitted, his voice barely above a whisper.

Rebecca placed a hand on his cheek, her touch grounding him. "You stop by letting people in. By letting us help you."

For the first time in weeks, Gavin felt the weight on his shoulders lighten, just a little. He nodded, allowing her to guide him back home.

Gavin woke to the stale smell of whiskey and regret. His head throbbed, a dull echo of the punches he'd traded the night before. He groaned, shifting on the creaking bed. The room was dim, its only light slipping through a crack in the faded curtains. A woman's figure moved in the periphery, and as she turned, Gavin recognized Rebecca. She stood by the basin, wringing out a damp cloth.

"Morning, sunshine," she said, her voice a mix of sarcasm and concern. She walked over and pressed the cloth to the cut on his cheek. He winced.

"Don't look so tough now, do you?" she added with a smirk.

"What happened?" he rasped.

"You got stupid, that's what. Picked a fight with a man twice your size. He'd have killed you if I hadn't dragged you out of there."

Gavin let his head fall back against the pillow, his chest tight with shame and anger. It had been weeks since Mike's death, and the anguish it brought pressed harder each day. Gavin had drifted aimlessly, drowning in liquor and bitterness, seeking solace in the chaos of saloons and brawls. The pain of loss and the guilt of survival gnawed at him, a constant ache he couldn't shake.

Rebecca sat on the edge of the bed, crossing her arms. Her sharp blue eyes softened slightly, though her tone remained firm. "You're lucky, you know that? Lucky to be alive. Mike ain't. And if you keep this up, you'll end up just like him."

"Maybe everyone would be better off," Gavin muttered, staring at the stained ceiling.

Rebecca's hand shot out, grabbing his chin and forcing him to look at her. "Don't you dare," she hissed. "You don't get to wallow and throw your life away like it means nothing. You think you're the only one who's had it rough?"

Gavin blinked, startled by the fire in her voice. She released him and stood, pacing the room as if trying to gather her thoughts.

"You think this is what I dreamed of?" she continued, gesturing to the shabby room. "Selling myself to men who can't even look me in the eye? This wasn't the plan, Gavin. I had a family once. Parents who kicked me out because I got pregnant out of wedlock. The father? He ran off the moment I told him. I lost everything. But I'm still here. I'm still fighting."

Her voice cracked, but she straightened her shoulders, defiance flashing in her eyes. "You, on the other hand, have the whole damn world in front of you. But you're too blind—too stupid—to see it. You're pissing it away on booze and bar fights."

Gavin sat up, her words cutting deeper than any blade. He tried to speak, but no sound came out.

Rebecca's gaze softened again as she approached him, placing a hand on his shoulder.

"I'm not saying it's easy," she said quietly. "But you've got to find something to live for. Otherwise, what's the point?"

Gavin lowered his head, her words sinking into the cracks of his armor. For so long, he had let his pain consume him, using it as an excuse to self-destruct. But Rebecca's story, her resilience, was a mirror he hadn't expected to face.

"What do I do?" he asked finally, his voice barely above a whisper.

Rebecca smiled faintly, her fingers brushing a strand of hair from his forehead. "Start by sobering up. And then... figure out what's next. You're good at running, Gavin. But maybe it's time to stop."

The silence that followed was heavy but not oppressive. Gavin nodded slowly, a flicker of determination sparking within him. He didn't know what his future held, but for the first time in a long while, he felt a glimmer of hope—thanks to Rebecca, the woman who had pulled him from the brink and reminded him that life, no matter how fractured, was still worth fighting for.

The time that followed blurred together in a mix of routine and quiet companionship. Rebecca's modest cottage became Gavin's refuge, a place to escape the ghosts that haunted him. Her son Joseph quickly grew attached to him, following him around and mimicking his every move. For the first time in a long while, Gavin felt a semblance of stability, but deep down, he knew it was fleeting.

Late one evening, as the house settled into silence, Gavin sat by the hearth, his thoughts swirling like smoke. Rebecca approached, her presence grounding but laced with unspoken tension.

"You've been restless lately," she said, sitting across from him.

Gavin sighed, running a hand over his face. "I've been trying to convince myself this is enough. That I can build something here. But the truth is, it's not. I don't love you, Rebecca. Not the way I should."

Rebecca's eyes flickered with understanding, though there was a trace of sadness. "You don't have to explain, Gavin. I knew from the start."

The silence between them was heavy but not bitter. Gavin leaned forward, his elbows resting on his knees. "I need to leave. Find out who I am. Become the man I should've been a long time ago."

Rebecca nodded, her voice steady despite the emotion in her eyes. "Then go. But don't leave without saying goodbye to Joseph. He looks up to you more than you realize."

"I will" was all he could muster. He knew that saying goodbye to Joseph was going to be the hardest part.

That night Rebecca took Gavin into her bed, the air between them charged with unspoken emotion. Their passion ignited, a fiery culmination of the bond they'd been building. She touched him with tenderness, and he responded with a fervor that surprised even himself. For a moment, he tried to believe he could belong here, that this could be enough, but he knew it was a fool's dream and that he didn't belong there with them.

Early the next morning, the house was quiet as Gavin packed his few belongings. He placed Mike's share of their stolen fortune on the kitchen table, a silent apology and a parting gift. Rebecca was still asleep, her auburn hair spilling over the pillow, peaceful in slumber.

As Gavin opened the front door, a small voice called out. "Gavin?"

He turned to see Joseph standing in the hallway, clutching a blanket, his eyes wide and glistening. The boy ran to him, wrapping his small arms around Gavin's leg.

"You're leaving?" Joseph's voice quivered with hurt.

Gavin knelt down, placing his hands on Joseph's shoulders. "I have to, kiddo. But you're the man of the house now. You've got to look after your mama and your aunt. Think you can do that?"

Joseph sniffled but nodded, his small face resolute. Gavin pulled a coin from his pocket—a rare token he'd always considered his lucky charm—and pressed it into Joseph's hand.

"Keep this for me," Gavin said with a faint smile.

"And here—" He placed his hat on the boy's head, the brim too large for Joseph's small frame. "You're in charge now."

Joseph clung to the coin and hat, his tears falling silently as Gavin stood and walked out the door. Mounting his horse, Gavin took one last look at the cottage. Then, with a deep breath, he spurred the horse eastward, the rising sun casting a golden glow over the horizon.

Gavin rode a day and night to Omaha where he sold off his horse and purchased a train ticket to Boston on the Union Pacific Railroad. He kept the money he had left, which was a significant amount, tucked into the bottom of his bag, the few clothes and other items nestled on top so as not to advertise to anyone the small fortune he was carrying. Having robbed as many banks as he had, he laughed to himself as he thought of opening an account to deposit what he had stolen from the very institutions he would soon request assistance.

CHAPTER 19

The journey eastward was long but it gave Gavin ample time to reflect. Each sunrise brought him closer to Boston, a place he'd heard about in fleeting conversations in saloons and from drifters. It was a city painted as a land of opportunity, of bustling harbors and streets teeming with life. But to Gavin, it was simply a place far enough from his past to offer a fresh start.

By the time he arrived, the city was alive with the energy of progress. The streets hummed with the clatter of horses' hooves and the rumble of carriages. Steam billowed from factory chimneys, and the air was heavy with the mingling scents of baked goods, salt from the harbor, and the unmistakable stench of too many people living too close together.

Gavin's first glimpse of Boston was through the fog of early morning. The harbor bustled with activity, ships of every size coming and going like busy bees. Sailors shouted commands as they unloaded crates of goods from distant lands. The docks were alive with merchants peddling everything from fresh fish to exotic spices.

After a regaining focus on the present and realizing he had more money than he knew what to do with slung over his shoulder, Gavin knew it wouldn't take long for him to get robbed. He approached a wealthy looking gentleman and asked him where he might find a bank. Not wanting to bring attention to himself, he told the man that he didn't have any money on him but needed to find the bank to make a withdrawal in order to secure lodgings. The gentleman directed Gavin to the Provident Institution for Savings on Tremont Street. After receiving some simple directions, Gavin made his way to the bank and found himself standing in the shadow of the impressive and newly constructed bank building, his hands trembling as he clutched his bag half filled with stolen money. The memories of his past actions pressed heavily on his conscience, but the moment had finally arrived. This was a turning point—a chance to reclaim his life.

The sun glared down from a cloudless sky as Gavin pushed himself off the dusty bench, his heart racing with anticipation and fear. He could still picture Mike's broad grin, his laughter echoing in the back of Gavin's mind like a bittersweet melody. They had lived by the gun, but today would mark the day Gavin would lay that life to rest.

As he stepped inside the financial institution, the familiar scent of polished wood and ink filled the air, mixing with the soft murmur of patrons conducting their business. Gavin's pulse quickened, and he felt out of place, as if the walls themselves remembered the shadows of his past.

He approached the counter, where a young teller, oblivious to his history, smiled brightly. "Good morning, sir! How can I assist you today?"

Gavin swallowed hard; his throat dry as he placed the sack on the counter. "I'd like to deposit this," he managed, his voice steady despite the storm of emotions swirling inside him.

The teller's smile faltered for just a moment, her eyes darting to the worn sack before looking back up at him. "Of course! Just a moment." She turned away, and Gavin's heart raced, the gravity of what he was doing sinking in.

This was it—the culmination of a lifetime of regret, the start of something new. He could feel the eyes of the bank's patrons on him, but he refused to be swayed. He was no longer the man who robbed banks; he was ready to be someone else entirely.

As the teller returned, she counted the money carefully, her fingers deftly sorting through the bills and coins. Gavin's hands clenched the edge of the counter as she spoke, her voice echoing in the silence. "This is quite a sum. Are you sure you want to deposit all of it?"

He nodded, a tightness forming in his chest. "Yes, young lady. I am."

For a fleeting moment as she inspected the bills and coins he had brought in, he thought she could see right through him, that she somehow sensed the weight of the blood-soaked past he carried. But as she processed the transaction, that moment passed, and he felt a sense of relief wash over him.

With each bill she slid across the counter, Gavin felt lighter. The echoes of Mike's laughter, the thrill of their robberies, all of it faded like a distant memory. The finality of his decision anchored him, reminding him of the life he longed to build—a life away from the shadows.

After the deposit was made, Gavin left the bank with a resolve he hadn't felt in years. The sun warmed his skin, and he drew in a deep breath of the fresh air. It was time to start anew, time to reclaim his life from the grip of his past. As he ventured further into the city, his eyes widened at the blend of old and new. Brick buildings stood firm against the push of modernity; their facades weathered but proud. The streets were a patchwork of languages — Irish, Italian, German — blending together into a chaotic symphony. Vendors called out their wares, and children darted between pedestrians, their laughter ringing out like bells.

In the following weeks, Gavin found a place to stay and work as a labourer at a steel mill. It was hard gruelling work, but he didn't seem to mind as he felt the pain was cleansing his spirit. The promise of progress and the rhythmic clatter of steel on steel soothed his restless spirit. Days were filled with sweat and labor, but each evening, as the sun set over the horizon, he felt a sense of purpose and belonging he hadn't known in years.

He worked hard, earning the respect of his fellow laborers as they built and formed the metal into tracks that would connect a vast, rugged land. With each piece forged and formed, Gavin felt a part of something greater than himself, a chance to contribute to the future of the country.

Years passed, and life settled into a rhythm that felt almost normal, though monotonous. He made friends among the men he worked with, their laughter echoing against the walls of the saloons and parlors as they shared tales of home and dreams of the future. Gavin buried the memories of his past, crafting a new identity as a hardworking laborer who found joy in the simple things—a hot meal, the camaraderie of friends, the beauty of the vast landscape stretching before him. On occasion his new life would bring him to a pub and he would indulge, however he had learned his lesson and tried to control himself as best he could.

Gavin's wanderings eventually brought him to a crowded tavern in the Irish quarter. It was there he met Peter Duffy, a stocky man with a thick brogue and a quick smile. Peter had arrived from County Cork,

Ireland, just two years prior and had already made himself at home in Boston. Over a shared bottle of whiskey, the two struck up a fast friendship.

"You've the look of a man who's been through hell," Peter remarked, clapping Gavin on the shoulder. "But you're of Irish ancestry, so that's nothing new, eh?"

Peter worked as a dockhand but had connections that extended far beyond the harbor. When Gavin mentioned he was getting bored at the mill and looking for something new, Peter's eyes lit up. "I've got just the thing for you, mate. A ship's setting sail in a week, bound for Africa and then India. They're short a few men. It'll be hard work, but it'll fill your pockets."

Before they set sail, Peter and Gavin sat on the docks, watching the sunset paint the water in hues of orange and gold. Gavin hesitated, then voiced a concern that had been gnawing at him. "Peter, I need to ask—this ship, it's not involved in slave trading, is it?"

Peter's expression darkened momentarily before softening. "No, lad. I wouldn't steer you wrong. The *Sea Serpent* deals in goods—spices, sugar, silk, furs. Honest trade, as far as any trade can be. The captain's got no stomach for the other business. You've my word on that. And we're in a free state you know. Slavery is no longer accepted in these parts."

Relieved, Gavin nodded. "Good. I couldn't be part of something like that."

"I'll take ye to the wharf tomorrow and make the

introductions." Peter offered.

The following morning Peter and Gavin made their way to the wharf. The wharves of Boston were bustling as always, with ships from around the world unloading goods and taking on new cargo. It was here, amidst the chaos of barrels, crates, and shouting sailors, that Peter found the opportunity he was looking for.

Peter had spent the past couple years on the waterfront, first as a deckhand and later as a stevedore. His reputation as a dependable worker and a man who knew the maritime business inside and out had earned him the respect of many ship captains. One such captain was Benjamin Briggs of the *Sea Serpent*, a sleek merchant vessel known for its long voyages to Africa and India.

Peter had heard from a dockworker friend that Captain Briggs was short on crew for the *Sea Serpent's* next journey. It was a dangerous voyage—weeks at sea, unpredictable weather, and the threat of disease—but it was also an opportunity.

Peter waited near the gangplank of the *Sea Serpent*, watching as supplies were loaded. He caught sight of Captain Briggs, a tall man with a weathered face and a sharp gaze, issuing orders to his men.

"Captain Briggs," Peter called out, stepping forward.

Briggs turned, his expression stern but curious. "What is it, Peter? You looking to sign on again?"

Peter shook his head. "Not for me this time,

Captain. I've got someone in mind for you. A strong lad, hard worker, and desperate for a chance."

Briggs raised an eyebrow. "Desperate, huh? I don't hire troublemakers."

"He's no troublemaker," Peter said quickly. "He's just… run into some hard times. Name's Gavin. He's got no sailing experience, but he's willing to learn. You know me, Captain—I wouldn't vouch for someone who was afraid of an honest day's work."

Briggs rubbed his chin, sizing Gavin up. "No experience, you say. You look to be a sturdy lad. Healthy, got all your teeth… Well, we've all got to start somewhere and I could use the extra set of hands. It'll take ya a few days to get your sea legs mind you and I won't start you off at the same rate as an experienced sailor."

Gavin nodded. "Thank you, Captain. You won't regret it."

Captain Briggs narrowed his gaze. "I'm sure, but a ship's no place for hesitation or second thoughts. Once you're aboard, you're part of the crew. You pull your weight, follow orders, and earn your keep. Understood?"

"Yes, sir," Gavin replied, his voice steady.

Briggs nodded. "Good. Report to the bosun. He'll find you a berth and get you started."

As Gavin stepped onto the gangplank, he took in the sight of his new abode. The *Sea Serpent*, was a three-masted barque, its sails a patchwork of repairs but sturdy enough for the long voyage ahead. Gavin joined the crew, finding himself among a motley group of sailors—some seasoned, others green as spring leaves. The captain, a wiry New Englander named Benjamin Briggs, ran a tight ship but treated his crew fairly.

Life aboard the *Sea Serpent* was grueling. Days were spent hauling lines, scrubbing decks, and repairing sails. The sea was both friend and foe, offering moments of serene beauty followed by bouts of violent tempests. Nights were filled with the creak of timber, the crash of waves, and the occasional song from a homesick sailor.

The journey took Gavin from the shores of West Africa to the sprawling expanse of Calcutta, a city as dazzling as it was overwhelming. After the humid coasts of Africa, where towering palms swayed over crowded ports and trade were a cacophony of shouts and haggling, the ship rounded the Cape of Good Hope. The seas were wild and treacherous, the waves battering the ship with relentless force. Gavin learned quickly to brace himself, to tie down every piece of cargo, and to navigate the slippery, lurching deck with the confidence of a seasoned sailor.

When the ship reached Calcutta, Gavin was unprepared for the sensory onslaught. The air clung to him like a second skin, heavy with the mingled scents of spices, sweat, and decay. The streets were a riot of color and noise—bright saris fluttered like butterflies, merchants touted their wares, and sacred cows wandered freely amid the chaos. Majestic colonial buildings loomed over labyrinthine alleyways teeming with life, their facades a stark reminder of the British Empire's grip on the land.

Unbeknownst to Gavin and the rest of the crew was that beneath the vibrant surface, unease simmered. Gavin heard whispers among the sailors and dockworkers, rumors of growing unrest. Sepoys—Indian soldiers serving under British command—were said to be on the brink of rebellion, their grievances rooted in religious offenses, cultural insensitivity, and systemic exploitation. The tension was palpable, a powder keg waiting for a spark.

It was much to the *Sea Serpent*'s misfortune that during their time docked in harbour, the rebellion began. The sepoys, galvanized by decades of oppression and the recent introduction of rifle cartridges rumored to be greased with cow and pig fat, rose in defiance. What started as mutiny spread like wildfire across the northern plains, engulfing villages and cities. Gavin's ship was stranded as the port descended into chaos. Supplies dwindled, and the sailors ventured inland, seeking refuge and sustenance in a land aflame with conflict.

The horrors Gavin witnessed would stay with him for the rest of his days. Villages were left in smoldering ruins, the charred remains of homes and fields stretching as far as the eye could see. Entire communities were decimated—men slaughtered, women violated, and children left orphaned or worse. The British reprisals were equally barbaric. Soldiers razed villages suspected of harboring rebels, their vengeance swift and indiscriminate.

Seeking to avoid desertion and the complete loss of his ship and cargo, Captain Briggs ordered all hands-on deck as they pulled anchor and moved to safer harbours, or so they thought.

In Cawnpore, Gavin came face to face with the aftermath of one of the most infamous atrocities of the rebellion. At Bibighar, the mutilated remains of British women and children were discovered, their bodies cast into a well. Gavin's stomach churned as he stood before the bloodied stones, the cries of survivors a haunting echo in the sweltering air.

Days later, he bore witness to British retribution. Suspected rebels were rounded up, bound, and tied to the muzzles of cannons. Gavin's ears rang with the deafening roar of the blasts as bodies were torn apart, blood raining down in a macabre spectacle. The smell of gunpowder mingled with the sickly stench of burning flesh, and Gavin felt his soul fracture under the horror of the violence.

Each step through the rebellion-torn land drove home the fragility of civilization. Gavin, once a man hardened by his own losses, found his heart cracking open to the sheer depth of human suffering.

Gavin could no longer tell where justice ended

and atrocity began. Both sides committed horrors so profound that the lines blurred into a haze of blood and fire. He watched as soldiers—British and Indian alike—became monsters in the name of loyalty, revenge, or survival. And yet, amid the carnage, there were moments of humanity: a mother shielding her child, a sepoy risking his life to lead a wounded stranger to safety, a British officer lowering his weapon in silent defiance of orders.

These flickers of goodness only deepened Gavin's despair. They were not enough to outweigh the darkness, the relentless cycle of violence that seemed to devour everything it touched. For the first time, he questioned whether humanity was worth saving at all.

When the rebellion was finally quashed, the *Sea Serpent* returned to sea, but Gavin, and the rest of the crew alike, were no longer the same men who had set out from Boston. The sea that had once seemed vast and freeing now felt like a prison, its horizon a cruel reminder of the limits of escape. He drifted through ports, haunted by the faces of the dead and the cries of the living. The world had shown him its ugliest face, and he could no longer look away.

He arrived in Boston months later. Tired from his journey, he found a room to stay in for the night. The city was alive around him. Fights in the street, laughing men, screaming girls, the odd gunshot and the sounds of people bustling about kept him up. He found himself once again in familiar territory.

Lost. He was no longer impressed by the city life. He yearned for a simpler life. It had been many years since he killed Ellis. He began to think of Marek and their family farm. The years had worn on his face and perhaps he would be able to walk amongst his former community members unnoticed. Perhaps those that meant to harm him had moved on or died.

By the time he resolved to return home to Maple Creek, Gavin carried a new kind of burden—not just the weight of his past sins, but the crushing realization that perhaps no place, no people, and no heart was free from the corruption he had seen. Yet, beneath the despair, a flicker of hope persisted, fragile, but insistent. Perhaps, in the land of his youth, he might find something to rekindle his faith—or at least, some measure of peace.

CHAPTER 20

One evening, as the sun dipped low on the horizon, painting the sky orange and red, Gavin sat by the railway tracks, the sound of the distant train echoing in the background. It was time. He needed to confront the ghosts of his past, to see if there was a place for him in the town he had once called home.

Upon returning to Boston, Gavin sought out the Provident Institution for Savings. The imposing granite building stood as a symbol of the city's growing prosperity, its polished brass fixtures and soaring ceilings exuding an air of trust and permanence. Gavin hesitated on the threshold, his weathered boots scuffing against the marble floor, before stepping inside with a determined stride.

Inside, clerks moved efficiently behind tall counters of dark wood, their hands deftly flipping through ledgers and counting bills. The air smelled faintly of ink and aged paper, a reminder of the business conducted within these walls. Gavin approached the counter and waited as a clerk, an older man with spectacles perched on the tip of his nose, finished assisting another client.

"Good day, sir," Gavin said when it was his turn, his voice steady despite the nature of his intentions. "I'd like to withdraw enough funds for a journey westward, and I'd also like to leave instructions regarding my account."

The clerk peered at Gavin over his spectacles, nodding slightly. "Very well, sir. May I have your account information?"

Gavin handed over a small leather-bound book containing his account details, acquired years ago when he first deposited his earnings from his voyage aboard the *Sea Serpent*. The clerk reviewed it briefly before gesturing to a nearby desk. "Please take a seat. I'll fetch the account ledger and inform the manager of your request."

Moments later, Gavin sat across from the institution's manager, a portly man with a carefully trimmed mustache and an aura of quiet authority. "I understand you'd like to make some significant changes to your account, Mr. Craite?" the manager asked.

"That's correct," Gavin replied. "I need to withdraw enough for my journey westward. But I also want to ensure that the remainder—what you'll find is a small fortune—is left in the account with clear instructions for access."

The manager nodded, gesturing to a clerk who returned with the large, leather-bound ledger of Gavin's account. As the ledger was placed before them, Gavin continued, "I want my brother, Marek Craite, to have full access to the account. Should Marek pass, or in his absence, his spouse and any children he may have, whose names I do not yet know, are to inherit the rights to the account."

The manager furrowed his brow, considering the unusual request. "This is possible, Mr. Craite, though it will require precise documentation. We'll need your written authorization to grant such access and your signature on several pages of the ledger. Additionally, you must designate Marek Craite as the primary beneficiary in our records. Do you have a trusted witness who can verify your identity?"

Gavin nodded. "My shipmate, Peter, can vouch for me."

With Peter called in as a witness, the process began. Gavin provided his signature on multiple forms, and Peter confirmed Gavin's identity under oath. The manager meticulously noted the details, ensuring the instructions for Marek and his family were clear and binding.

"One last thing, Mr. Craite," the manager said. "Should Marek or his family ever need to access the funds, they will need to present identification, or a trusted legal representative may come on their behalf. We will keep this arrangement on file and ensure its integrity."

Satisfied, Gavin withdrew the amount he needed for his journey, the crisp banknotes tucked safely into his coat. As he left the Provident Institution for Savings, he glanced back at the granite façade, feeling a sense of closure. He had ensured that his fortune would not wither but instead serve as a lifeline for the brother who had stood by him through his darkest days.

Traveling west in the late 1870s was no small feat, but the expanding rail network made it possible. Gavin first booked a ticket on the Boston and Albany Railroad, which carried him through the rolling hills of Massachusetts and into the bustling hub of Albany, New York. From there, he connected to the New York Central and Hudson River Railroad, traveling west to Chicago.

Chicago was a revelation. The city buzzed with industry, its skyline pierced by smokestacks and the occasional church steeple. The stockyards stretched endlessly, and the air was heavy with the smell of progress and livestock. After a brief layover, Gavin boarded the Chicago, Burlington and Quincy Railroad, heading northwest toward St. Paul, Minnesota.

From St. Paul, he switched to the Northern Pacific Railway, which carried him across the vast prairies. The golden expanse of the Great Plains stretched endlessly, broken only by the occasional herd of bison or a distant cluster of trees. Towns were few and far between—simple collections of wooden buildings huddled against the wind.

At Bismarck, in the Dakota Territory, Gavin had to arrange for a horse to complete the final leg of his journey. Rail lines had yet to reach the remote borderlands near Montana and the Northwest Territory, and the open plains required a sturdy mount and a resilient spirit. He followed the Missouri River westward until he reached Fort Benton, Montana, a rugged frontier town that served as a key trading post.

Fort Benton marked the last taste of civilization before the wilderness. From there, Gavin rode north, crossing into Canada near the Cypress Hills. The land became familiar as he approached Maple Creek, its rolling hills and endless skies stirring memories of a simpler time. The sight of the old farmstead in the distance brought a pang to his chest. It was here that he hoped to reconcile with his past, to find a sense of purpose amid the scars of his journey. Memories flooded back—scenes of his childhood, laughter shared with Marek, the bittersweet taste of first love with Shannon. Each mile was a step closer to reconciling with the man he had become and the life he had left behind.

The town appeared on the horizon, a ghost of a memory but one that held the potential for redemption. Gavin's heart raced as he approached, uncertainty mingling with hope. Would Marek still be there? Would he welcome him back, or had too much time passed?

As he entered the town, Gavin felt the weight of his past lifting slightly, replaced by a sense of determination. He was no longer the frightened young man who had fled in the darkness; he was a survivor, a man shaped by loss and hardship, ready to embrace whatever awaited him.

With a deep breath, Gavin stepped into the town he once knew, ready to face the ghosts of his past and hopefully forge a new path forward.

CHAPTER 21

Gavin Craite stood at the crest of the hill overlooking the farm that had shaped his boyhood. The air was thick with the scent of earth and hay, tinged faintly with the pine from the surrounding forest. Below, the sun dipped low in the sky, casting a golden glow over the weathered farmhouse and fields. Memories came rushing back—his mother calling him and Marek in for supper, the laughter they shared over chores, and the boundless innocence of youth. His heart pounded as he stood frozen in place, torn between joy and trepidation.

The path to the homestead felt longer than he remembered, as though the weight of years slowed his steps. The porch creaked beneath his boots, the sound both familiar and haunting. Yet something felt off. The farm was in better shape than when he had left it—fresh paint on the house, fences mended, and the fields cleared. Two dogs appeared from the yard, bounding toward him with sharp barks and low growls, their bodies tense with suspicion. Gavin stopped, raising his hands calmly.

"Easy, now," he murmured, his voice steady but kind. The dogs slowed, sniffing the air, their ears twitching before deciding he was no threat. They retreated with watchful eyes, still wary but no longer hostile.

The rhythmic 'thunk' of an axe striking wood drifted from the far side of the house, drawing Gavin's attention. He rounded the corner, his boots crunching over gravel and dirt, and saw a figure by the treeline. The young man was chopping wood with steady precision, each swing splitting the logs cleanly.

"Howdy," Gavin called out, his voice breaking the quiet evening.

The young man froze mid-swing, the axe buried deep in a log. Slowly, he turned, wiping sweat from his brow with a forearm. His lean frame was backlit by the setting sun, the light framing his figure in a warm halo. For a moment, his expression was neutral, but then it shifted—a flicker of recognition mixed with wariness.

"Who are you?" the young man asked, his voice steady but tinged with caution.

Gavin stepped closer, keeping his movements deliberate and unthreatening. "Name's Gavin Craite. I grew up here."

The young man looked shocked, his grip tightening on the axe handle. "Gavin? Marek Craite's brother?"

"That's right." Gavin smiled faintly, though his chest tightened. "You know him?"

The young man nodded slowly. "He's my pa."

The words hit Gavin like a blow. He blinked, his breath catching as he took in the young man before him—a younger version of Marek, with the same determined set of the jaw and intense eyes. "You're... you're his son."

The young man nodded again. "Finnian Craite. Folks call me Finn."

Gavin's voice was hoarse when he spoke. "Well, Finn, where's your pa? Is he around?"

Finn glanced toward the house, his expression guarded. "He's inside. Not sure how he'll take to seeing you. Been a long time, and... well, folks said you were dead."

Gavin swallowed hard. "I reckon he'll be surprised. But I can assure you... I'm ain't dead."

Finn studied Gavin for a moment, then nodded toward the house. "Come along then, I'll take ya to the house and we'll give Da' a heart attack."

Gavin felt his heart beating fast in his chest. He had come this far. Whatever happened next, he was ready.

Gavin followed Finn toward the house, the young man chatting easily as they walked. "You're a bit of a legend around here, you know," Finn said, glancing back with a grin.

"A legend?" Gavin repeated, his face looking surprised.

"Yeah," Finn said. "Da's told us stories about you—how you were always the wild one, getting into trouble but somehow coming out on top." He laughed lightly. "I guess I've got a bit to live up to, but coming out on top would not be how I would describe it."

Gavin smiled faintly, though the mention of Marek tugged at something deep inside him. "He's always been the better storyteller."

Finn shrugged, his eyes sparkling with curiosity. "Maybe, but he always made you sound like a hero."

Before Gavin could respond, they reached the porch. A girl—Makenna, Finn had called her—was waiting there. "Who's your friend?" she asked Finn.

"You won't believe me if I told ya, but this is Da's brother, our Uncle Gavin," Finn explained.

Makenna tilted her head, studying him with sharp, inquisitive eyes.

"No. You're kidding. So, you're the famous Uncle Gavin? I thought you were dead." she said, crossing her arms with a playful smirk. "Da's got loads of stories about you."

Gavin chuckled, his chest tightening at the familiarity in her expression. "All good ones, I hope."

"Depends who's telling them," Makenna shot back, her grin widening.

Before he could press further, the door opened,

and Marek stepped out. Gavin's heart skipped a beat at the sight of his brother, older now but still carrying that air of calm and reliability. Marek's eyes widened as he took in the sight of Gavin, and then, without hesitation, he crossed the porch and pulled him into a tight hug.

Marek's face lit up with surprise and then confusion. "Gavin? Is that really you?"

"Marek," Gavin replied, his voice thick with a mix of emotions. "I'm back. God, I missed ya."

"After all these years… We thought you'd—But you're here," Marek started but stopped short, his eyes darting away.

"I'm here," Gavin murmured, his throat constricting. He clapped Marek on the back, the years of distance melting away for a brief moment. "It's been too long, brother."

Marek pulled back, his hands resting on Gavin's shoulders as he looked him over. "You look good," he said, though there was a flicker of unease in his expression.

"And you've got a farm that looks better than I ever remember it," Gavin replied with a grin, though his gaze drifted to Finn and Makenna. "And kids, apparently."

Marek's smile faltered ever so slightly. "Yeah," he said, clearing his throat. "Look, why don't we step inside? We've got some catching up to do."

Gavin nodded, though his curiosity simmered just

below the surface. As they stepped into the house, Marek gestured for the kids to stay outside. "Give us a bit, yeah?"

Finn and Makenna exchanged a glance, but they didn't argue. Marek led Gavin into the sitting room, where a fire crackled in the hearth. He poured them both a glass of whiskey, handing one to Gavin before sitting down heavily in a chair.

As the brothers sat there, Gavin looked out a large window, his gaze sweeping over the farm that felt both familiar and foreign. Marek remained quiet, watching him, the silence between them thick with unspoken words. Finally, Gavin broke it.

"And Pa?" Gavin asked, his voice low, as if the question carried a pain he wasn't sure he wanted to bear.

Marek sighed, folding his arms across his chest. "He passed, Gavin. A year or so after you left."

Gavin's lips pressed into a thin line, his eyes shifting to the horizon. "Figured as much. He wasn't exactly the picture of health when I left."

"No, he wasn't," Marek admitted, his tone neutral. "After Ma died, he just… broke. Whatever part of him that held us together fell apart with her. He started drinking more, working less. You know how he was."

Gavin nodded, the memories of their father's sharp words and heavier hand flashing through his mind. "Yeah, I know." He hesitated, then added, "I always thought if I stayed, maybe… maybe he'd have straightened out."

Marek shook his head, a wry smile tugging at the corner of his mouth. "You couldn't have fixed him, Gavin. None of us could. He was already too far gone by then."

"Did he suffer?" Gavin asked, glancing at Marek.

"Not much," Marek replied. "One night, he went to bed after drinking himself blind and just didn't wake up. Peaceful, if you can call it that."

"Where'd you bury him?"

Marek gestured toward the tree line in the distance. "By the creek, next to Ma. Figured it was the least I could do for him."

Gavin let out a bitter laugh. "Least you could do? You gave him more than he ever gave us after she died."

Marek shrugged; his gaze distant. "Maybe. But I didn't bury him there for his sake, Gavin. I did it for her. She wouldn't have wanted him tossed in some unmarked grave like a stranger."

For a moment, they stood in silence, the bond of their shared past settling between them. Gavin's jaw tightened, and he swallowed hard. "I still see her sometimes," he said quietly. "In my dreams. The way she smiled, the way she'd hum when she was baking bread."

"Me too," Marek said, his voice softening. "She was the best of us, wasn't she?"

Gavin nodded. "Aye, she was." He glanced at

Marek, his expression softening. "You did right by her, Marek. You always did."

Marek looked at him, a flicker of emotion passing across his face before he smiled faintly. "We all did what we could, Gavin. And now, here we are."

"Here we are," Gavin echoed, though the words felt heavier than he intended. He looked out the open window, where the whispers and muffled laughter of Finn and Makenna spilled through.

Marek placed a hand on Gavin's shoulder, his grip firm. "It's good to have you back, brother."

"It's good to be back," Gavin replied, though a strange feeling churned in his chest, as if the farm held secrets waiting to be unearthed. "So," Gavin began, swirling the whiskey in his glass. "You got married while I was gone?"

Marek hesitated, then took a long sip of his drink. "Yeah, sort of."

"Sort of?" Gavin raised an eyebrow. "What, you marry a woman who already had a family?"

Marek's jaw tightened, and he set his glass down on the table. "Well, yeah as a matter of fact…Gavin… it's uh, it's complicated."

"Complicated how?" Gavin asked, leaning forward. "You've got two great kids out there, and you're being all cagey about it."

Marek opened his mouth to reply but froze, his eyes darting toward the doorway. Gavin followed his gaze—and his breath caught in his throat.

"That's because they're yours," said a voice that came from the entrance to the room. A familiar voice. One that brought Gavin back to when he was a young man, living in a simpler time.

There, like a dream, standing in the doorway, was Shannon.

CHAPTER 22

avin stood up, staring at Shannon as though she were a ghost. In many ways to Gavin, she was just that.

Gavin looked at her "What... I... How? Why? What the hell is going on? You told me she was dead! You told me my child was, my children??? Were dead!" Gavin turned on his heels to face Marek.

"Gavin," Marek interrupted, stepping back and closing the door slightly. "You don't know the whole story. You have to understand—"

"Understand what? That you've kept me away for years? That you've lied to me?" Gavin felt anger swell within him, a tide threatening to drown out reason. "You told me Shannon and our baby died. Why would you do that?"

Marek's expression turned somber, and he ran a hand through his hair, a nervous habit Gavin recognized all too well. "It was to protect you," he finally admitted, his voice low. "It was Shannon's idea."

"Protect *me*?" Gavin echoed, disbelief flooding his veins. "You think lying to me for two decades was protecting me? I could have been there for her! For our kids!"

Marek shook his head, stepping closer, urgency etched in his features. "You don't know what happened, Gavin! When you killed Ellis, things got worse. His father, Bill, was furious. He was hunting for you. He would have killed you on sight. We couldn't let you come back and get yourself killed."

Gavin felt the weight of Marek's words sink in, but the anger didn't dissipate. "And so, you thought it best to keep me in the dark? How could you do that to me, Marek? To us?"

"Because Shannon made me swear I would do it and, if I'm being honest, I agreed with her." Marek confessed, his voice breaking. "I couldn't let her suffer. I married her, Gavin. I raised your children as my own."

At those words, Gavin's heart dropped. The revelation hit him like a bullet. He felt a whirlwind of emotions crash over him—rage, betrayal, but also a flicker of something else, something deeper and more complex.

"If you're being honest? That doesn't have the meaning it might once have had. Your children..." Gavin whispered, the realization striking him. "You lied to me about everything."

"Gavin, it was Shannon's choice," Marek said, his voice steady. "She thought it best for everyone involved. I never wanted to take your place. But she was terrified of the danger you faced. She loved you too much to see you get hurt."

Gavin stepped back, struggling to process the truth. He had imagined this reunion many times in his dreams, a fantasy, never once considering the path his life had taken was a fool's errand. "And you followed through on her idea? You took my place in her life?"

"I did what I had to do!" Marek replied, the pain evident in his voice. "You were gone. We didn't know if you would ever return. It was a matter of survival, Gavin. For all of us. Shannon's father disowned her when he found out she was pregnant out of wedlock, and she turned up at our door. What was I supposed to do?"

"You were supposed to be my brother! You were supposed to let me make my own choices! You robbed me of my dream and you took the one thing I ever loved so much, for yourself."

"Gavin, it was never like that. I don't even like her, I mean, I like her as a person, but Gavin, I don't like women, not in the way you do." Marek protested.

"What are you talking about?" Gavin asked with a confused look on his face.

"I'm more inclined to dance with a man than a woman. Can we leave it at that?" Marek insisted.

Gavin closed his eyes, grappling with the conflicting emotions swirling inside him. A part of him wanted to scream at Marek, to rail against the betrayal. But another part understood the desperation that had driven his brother to make such a choice.

"Did you ever love me?" Gavin asked looking at Shannon, his voice barely above a whisper.

"More than you will know." She replied tears willing in her eyes.

The pain in Gavin's chest tightened, the consequences of the past threatening to crush him. "And what about our children? Do they know?"

"Finn and Makenna know that Marek is their father, because Marek is their father and he's been an amazing one at that." Shannon replied, a mix of pride and sorrow in her eyes. "They're good kids. Smart, curious and brave—they're just like you."

Gavin's heart swelled at the thought of a son and a daughter he had never known, children who carried his blood. "What do I do now? Do we tell them the truth?"

"That's up to you two. They're old enough now to know the truth and I don't want to take any more from you than I already have," said Marek.

Marek cleared his throat, breaking the heavy silence that had fallen over the room. He shifted his weight from one foot to the other, looking between Shannon and Gavin. "I'll leave you two to… catch up," he said, his voice steady but tinged with unease.

Gavin barely heard him, his eyes fixed on Shannon, as if afraid she might vanish if he looked away.

"I'll go find the kids, help them with their chores," Marek added, his tone lighter now, though his gaze lingered on Shannon for a moment longer than necessary. "They're probably off getting into trouble somewhere."

Shannon gave him a grateful nod. "Thank you, Marek."

He tipped his head in acknowledgment and stepped toward the door. As he opened it, the warm afternoon sunlight spilled into the room, cutting across the worn floorboards. "Gavin," he said, pausing, "don't scare her off, yeah?" His smile was soft, teasing, but his eyes carried an unspoken pain.

Gavin didn't respond, still rooted in place. Marek left, closing the door quietly behind him, leaving the two of them alone.

For a moment, neither of them spoke. Gavin took a hesitant step forward, his hands twitching at his sides as if unsure whether to reach for her. "Shannon," he finally said, his voice raw and trembling.

Her name on his lips was a lifeline, something he had whispered in the dark for years, a prayer he thought would never be answered.

She smiled at him, though her eyes glistened with unshed tears. "It's really you," she said softly, her voice catching on the words.

Gavin's breath hitched as he stepped closer, still

hesitant, as though touching her might shatter the fragile reality of the moment. "I—I thought you were gone," he stammered, his voice thick with emotion. "Marek told me you… he said you and the baby…" He couldn't finish the sentence, the words too heavy to say aloud.

Shannon's smile faltered, and she looked down, wringing her hands. "I thought I'd never see you again," she whispered. "Not after what happened. Not after Marek told me you left."

Gavin's knees felt weak as he crossed the space between them in two strides. "Left? Shannon, I didn't leave because I wanted to," he said, his voice breaking. "I had to. I didn't know—God, I didn't know you were still here. That you were alive. That…" He trailed off, his eyes searching hers, pleading for answers.

Tears began to fall down her cheeks, and she let out a shaky breath. "I thought you'd never come back, Gavin. I thought I'd lost you forever."

He reached out then, cupping her face with trembling hands. His touch was tentative at first, as if afraid she might disappear like a ghost. But she leaned into him, her hands coming up to grasp his wrists.

"You didn't lose me," he said fiercely. "You didn't lose me. I thought I lost you. Shannon, I mourned you every day. I—" His voice broke, and he pulled her into his arms, holding her tightly as if to make up for all the years they had been apart.

She clung to him just as tightly, her tears soaking

into his shirt. "I never stopped loving you, Gavin," she choked out. "Not for a single second."

His chest ached at her words, and he buried his face in her hair, inhaling the familiar scent of her that he thought he'd never experience again. "I love you," he murmured, his voice rough and unsteady. "I always have. I never stopped, Shannon."

They pulled back slightly, just enough for their eyes to meet. The distance between them seemed to vanish as their lips met in a kiss that was both desperate and tender, a collision of years of longing and the relief of finally being together again.

The world around them seemed to fall away, as it had once before on the dance floor all those years ago. And for that moment, there was nothing but the two of them. No years of pain, no lies, no distance—just the love they had thought was lost and now found again.

When they finally broke apart, Shannon rested her forehead against his, her tears mixing with his. "There's so much we need to talk about," she said softly, her voice barely above a whisper.

"There's time," Gavin replied, his hands still cradling her face. "All I care about right now is that you're here. That you're alive. That we've got this moment."

She nodded, her lips trembling as she tried to smile. "I've waited so long for this."

"So have I," he said, brushing a strand of hair from

her face.

Outside, the faint sound of Marek's laughter with the children drifted through the open window, a reminder that the world still turned, even in moments like this. But for Gavin and Shannon, time had stopped, and they were finally where they belonged—together.

CHAPTER 23

The soft creak of the stairs announced Gavin and Shannon's return from the upstairs bedroom. Finn glanced up from the table where he was peeling potatoes and exchanged a puzzled look with Makenna. It wasn't unusual for their mother to retreat to her room, but seeing her come down with Gavin, of all people, was something new.

"About time," Marek said lightly from where he stood by the hearth, stirring the stew-pot. "We're starving here, and these two", he gestured toward the twins "are about as useful in the kitchen as a pair of cats."

Finn rolled his eyes. "We're peeling the potatoes, aren't we?"

"Barely," Marek teased, then turned back to his work.

Gavin and Shannon exchanged a brief, almost shy

glance before Shannon moved toward the table to help set it. Gavin trailed after her, his eyes never straying far from her as though he couldn't quite believe she was there. Makenna noticed, narrowing her eyes slightly. Something about the way they looked at each other, like there was a conversation happening silently between them, felt…off.

The awkwardness carried into supper. They all sat around the table, passing dishes of stew, bread, and greens. Marek kept up his usual banter, poking fun at Finn's appetite and Makenna's stubbornness, but there was a tension in the air that no amount of joking could dispel.

It wasn't just the furtive glances between Shannon and Gavin. It was the way their hands brushed when reaching for the same dish, the way Shannon laughed just a little too easily at something Gavin said, and the way he leaned in when she spoke.

Marek finally cleared his throat, breaking the uncomfortable silence. "Perhaps you two should remember who's at the table," he said, his tone light but pointed. His gaze flicked between Shannon and Gavin.

Shannon's cheeks flushed, and she quickly looked down at her plate. Gavin coughed, suddenly very interested in his stew.

But Makenna wasn't about to let it slide. She slammed her fork down onto the table, the sound echoing in the room. "All right, that's enough," she said sharply, her green eyes flashing.

"Makenna," Finn warned, his voice low.

"No," she snapped, turning to her mother. "What do you think you're doing? Sitting here, carrying on like that—like he's your—" She gestured at Gavin, her words catching in her throat. "It's disgraceful, Mother. Acting this way right in front of Father."

"Makenna!" Marek's voice was firm, but there was an edge of discomfort in it.

Shannon's face turned pale, her hands clutching the edge of the table. "It's not what you think—"

"Oh, isn't it?" Makenna shot back. "You think we don't see it? The way you're looking at him; the way you're acting?" She turned her anger toward Gavin. "And you! You're supposed to be Pa's brother! How can you sit there and—"

"That's enough!" Marek's voice cut through the room like a blade. Everyone froze, the weight of his authority settling over them.

Finn looked between his sister and his uncle; his mind was searching for clarity amongst the confusion. "What's going on?"

Marek took a deep breath, his expression pained. "This isn't the time, Makenna. Or the place."

But Makenna wasn't backing down. "Then, when is the time? When she's run off with him? When she—"

"Enough!" Shannon's voice, trembling but firm, silenced the room. Her hands were shaking as she gripped the table. "You don't understand, Makenna.

Neither of you do."

Gavin reached for her hand, but she pulled away, standing abruptly. "Marek, I can't—"

Marek stood as well, his face a mask of controlled frustration. "You don't have to explain anything, Shannon." He turned to Makenna and Finn, his tone softening. "Finish your supper. We'll talk later."

But the damage was done. The twins exchanged bewildered and hurt glances as Shannon fled the room, tears glistening in her eyes. Gavin hesitated, torn between following her and staying, but Marek's warning gaze kept him in his seat.

"I don't know what's going on," Finn said quietly, breaking the silence, "but I think we deserve to know."

Marek sighed, running a hand through his hair. "And you will. Soon." He looked to Gavin, his expression unreadable. "But not like this."

Makenna's gaze hardened. "It doesn't matter when. It's still wrong."

Gavin finally spoke, his voice low and steady. "It's not what you think, Makenna."

"Then what is it?" she demanded.

Gavin's jaw tightened, but he didn't answer. Marek placed a hand on his shoulder, a silent plea for patience.

"Eat your supper," Marek said quietly, his tone leaving no room for argument.

Reluctantly, Makenna and Finn picked up their forks, but the meal continued in strained silence, the storm of emotions brewing just beneath the surface, waiting to break.

After supper, the tension lingered in the air, thick as smoke. Shannon had not returned, leaving Marek to shuffle the dishes to the sink with Finn and Makenna reluctantly following suit. Gavin remained at the table, staring into the remnants of his stew as if they might offer answers.

Marek glanced at him, then at the twins, who were wordlessly scraping plates. "Go finish up outside," he said to them. "The chickens need shutting in, and the cows won't milk themselves."

Makenna opened her mouth to protest but caught the warning in Marek's eyes and thought better of it. Finn didn't need telling twice—he grabbed his coat and headed for the door, his sister trailing behind with a muttered, "I'm not done with this."

The door swung shut, leaving Marek and Gavin alone in the dimly lit kitchen. The clatter of dishes in the washbasin was the only sound for a moment. Marek leaned against the counter, arms crossed, and looked at his brother.

"That went about as well as I expected," Marek said dryly.

Gavin looked up, ashamed. "I didn't mean to cause trouble."

Marek sighed, rubbing a hand over his face. "I know. But it was bound to come to this sooner or later. They're not blind, Gavin. They see the way you and Shannon—" He stopped himself, shaking his head.

Gavin pushed back from the table and stood; his fists clenched at his sides. "I didn't come here to disrupt your life. I didn't even know—"

"I know you didn't." Marek's voice softened. "But now that you're here, things are…complicated."

Gavin let out a bitter laugh. "Complicated? Marek, everything about this is complicated. I'm standing in a house I thought I'd never see again, with a woman I thought was dead, and two children—" He stopped, his voice catching.

Marek looked away, the guilt on his face unmistakable.

Gavin took a step closer. "Why didn't you tell me?"

Marek met his gaze, his expression hardening. "Because you would've stayed."

"You're damn right I would've stayed!" Gavin's voice rose, echoing off the walls. "I would've faced whatever came for me if I'd known—"

"And gotten yourself killed!" Marek snapped, pushing off the counter. "Do you think Ellis' father would've let you live, even if you'd turned yourself in? I did what I had to do to protect you, Gavin. To protect her."

Gavin's shoulders sagged, the fight draining out of him. He sank back into his chair, running a hand through his hair. "And Shannon? Did she really know what you told me?"

Marek hesitated, then shook his head. "Gavin, it was her idea. She made me swear to tell you they were dead. She didn't want anything to happen to you; she loves you."

Gavin closed his eyes, the sincerity of Marek's words pressing down on him. "And the twins?"

Marek's jaw tightened. "I raised them as my own. They don't know any different."

Gavin looked up, his eyes filled with a mixture of gratitude and anguish. "You've done right by them. By her. I can't thank you enough for that."

Marek's expression softened, a flicker of sadness crossing his face. "I didn't do it for thanks, Gavin. I did it because I couldn't let her go through it alone. And because I love you."

The words hung in the air, raw and unspoken for years.

Gavin swallowed hard, nodding. "I don't know how to fix this, Marek."

Marek placed a hand on his brother's shoulder, his grip firm. "We'll figure it out. But for now, take it slow. They've lived their whole lives thinking I'm their father. This isn't something we can just drop on them over supper."

Gavin nodded again; his throat tight. "I'll follow your lead. Just…promise me we won't keep it from them forever."

"I promise," Marek said quietly. "But not tonight."

The door creaked open, and Finn poked his head in. "You coming, Uncle Gavin? Makenna's taking bets on whether you can still milk a cow."

Gavin managed a faint smile. "I'll be right there."

Finn gave a shrug and disappeared back into the night.

Marek gave Gavin's shoulder a squeeze. "Go. Try to act normal for a little while. Lord knows we'll need all the time we can get to figure this mess out."

Gavin nodded, grabbing his coat. As he stepped outside, he looked back at Marek, who stood in the doorway, watching him with a mixture of hope and worry.

The night air was cool, and the laughter of the twins carried through the yard. For a moment, Gavin allowed himself to believe that things might be okay. But deep down, he knew the hardest part was yet to come.

***

After a few days, it was time. Marek stepped onto the porch; his face shadowed but his posture steady. Shannon followed; her hands clasped tightly in front of her as though holding herself together. The firelight flickered behind them, casting a warm glow on the scene, but it did little to calm the storm brewing inside Gavin.

"Finn, Makenna," Marek called softly. The twins turned toward him, their smiles fading as they caught the somber tone in their father's voice. "Come inside. There's something we need to talk about."

The twins exchanged glances; their youthful energy

dampened by the weight in Marek's words. They followed him and Shannon into the parlour, where Gavin already sat, his hands resting on his knees, his expression unreadable.

"Is everything okay?" Makenna asked, her voice hesitant as she perched on the edge of the couch beside her brother.

Marek nodded but didn't sit. He paced to the fireplace, staring into the flames for a moment before turning back to face them. "You two are old enough now to know the truth about something important. Something we should have told you a long time ago."

Finn frowned, his gaze darting between the adults. "What truth? You're scaring us."

Shannon sat beside Gavin, her hand brushing his for reassurance. "We didn't tell you sooner because... well, it was complicated. We thought it was for the best. But you deserve to know now."

The room seemed to hold its breath as Marek spoke again, his voice steady but filled with emotion. "Gavin isn't just your uncle. He's your father. Your biological father."

The words hung in the air like a thunderclap.

Finn leaned back, his face pale, his mouth slightly open as though trying to form words. Makenna blinked rapidly, her brow furrowing as the revelation sank in.

"Wait—what?" Makenna finally managed. She looked from Marek to Shannon, then to Gavin, who was staring at the floor, his jaw tight. "How...how is that possible? Why didn't you tell us?"

Shannon reached for her daughter's hand, her own trembling. "It's a long story, sweetheart. But the most important thing to know is that we love you. All of us. That has never changed."

Finn shook his head, his voice shaking. "So, you raised us, Da, even though...?"

"I raised you because you're my family," Marek said firmly, stepping closer. "It didn't matter whose blood runs through your veins. You're my son and my daughter. That will never change."

Gavin finally lifted his head, his voice hoarse but resolute. "I know this is a lot to take in. And I don't expect you to understand everything right away. But I want you to know I never stopped thinking about you. Not for a single day."

Makenna's voice softened, though confusion still clouded her expression. "Why did you leave? Why didn't you stay?"

Gavin glanced at Marek and Shannon, a silent agreement passing between them. "It's...complicated. There were things I had to do, choices I had to make. But it wasn't because I didn't care. It was because I didn't know."

The twins sat in silence for a moment, their expressions a mixture of shock, hurt, and tentative understanding. Finally, Finn spoke, his voice quiet but steady. "It's a lot. But...I guess it doesn't change who we are. Or how we feel about any of you."

Makenna nodded, tears glistening in her eyes. "Yeah. It's just...a lot to process."

A tentative smile flickered across Shannon's face, and Marek's shoulders seemed to relax slightly. Gavin's chest ached with a mix of relief and lingering guilt, but for the first time in years, he felt a glimmer of hope.

As the night deepened, the family sat together, the bonds they shared reaffirmed and redefined. There were still questions, still emotions to untangle, but they faced them together, knowing that love—not blood—was what truly made them a family.

The following days at the farm passed in a rare kind of peace, the kind that felt fragile and precious, as though everyone knew it couldn't last forever. The tension of secrets revealed had dissipated, leaving a strange calm in its place.

Gavin spent his mornings working alongside Finn and Makenna, showing them old tricks of the trade he'd learned in his youth, while Marek oversaw the farm's operations with his usual quiet efficiency. Shannon would hum softly as she moved about the kitchen or tended to the garden, her eyes often straying to Gavin with a warmth that hadn't dimmed despite the years apart.

The twins had taken the revelation about Gavin being their father in stride, though not without questions.

"So," Finn had said over supper a few nights ago,

"you ran because of some trouble with the law?"

Gavin had hesitated, glancing at Shannon for reassurance. Her gentle nod gave him the courage to speak. "I made a mistake, Finn. A bad one. I thought leaving was the only way to protect your mother. And you."

Makenna had leaned forward, her sharp eyes narrowing. "What kind of mistake?"

"That's a story for another day," Marek had interjected smoothly, sensing the discomfort of the conversation pressing too heavily on everyone's shoulders. "For now, maybe we just focus on the fact that he's here."

And so, they did.

One sunny afternoon, Gavin and Shannon walked hand in hand through the fields, their steps slow and unhurried. The world around them was alive with the sounds of summer—birds chirping in the trees, the rustle of leaves in the breeze, the distant laughter of Finn and Makenna as they worked on repairing a section of the barn.

Shannon stopped beneath an old oak tree, her eyes shining as she turned to Gavin. "I can't believe you're here. That we're here."

Gavin cupped her face in his hands, his thumb brushing over her cheek. "Not a day went by that I didn't think of you, wonder if you were all right.... if you were happy."

"I wasn't," she admitted, her voice trembling. "Not

until now."

He kissed her then, slow and deep, as if making up for every kiss they'd missed over the years. When they pulled apart, Shannon rested her head against his chest, listening to the steady beat of his heart.

"What happens next?" she asked softly.

Gavin wrapped his arms around her, holding her close. "We take it one day at a time. I'm not going anywhere again, Shannon. Not unless you ask me to."

She smiled, though tears glistened in her eyes. "I'd never ask you to leave."

At the supper table that evening, the mood was light. Marek shared a story about a particularly stubborn cow that had taken a liking to the garden's lettuce patch, and Finn and Makenna laughed as they recounted their failed attempt to chase it off earlier in the day.

Gavin watched his children with a quiet pride, marveling at their resilience and spirit. He caught Shannon's eye across the table, and they shared a smile that spoke volumes.

Marek cleared his throat, drawing everyone's attention. "I think it's safe to say the farm's never run smoother. Having an extra pair of hands around has been good for us."

Finn smirked. "Not just hands. Uncle Gavin's got a good set of stories too."

"Don't encourage him," Marek said with mock exasperation.

Gavin chuckled, leaning back in his chair. "Careful, Marek. They might start calling me the storyteller of the family."

Makenna rolled her eyes but smiled. "That title's already taken by Mama."

Shannon laughed, her cheeks pink. "I think we can share it."

The sound of their laughter filled the room, and for a moment, everything felt perfect. But beneath the surface, Gavin couldn't shake the feeling that this peace was too good to last.

For now, though, he allowed himself to bask in it, savoring every fleeting moment with his family.

CHAPTER 24

The morning sun stretched across the open plains, bathing the farm in golden light as Gavin hitched the wagon to a team of sturdy horses. The air was crisp, filled with the earthy scent of hay and the faint murmur of cattle in the distance. Marek leaned against the fence, arms crossed, his brow furrowed as he watched Gavin tighten the straps.

"You sure about this?" Marek asked, his tone skeptical. "It's one thing to lay low here, but going into town... that's a risk."

Gavin smirked, wiping his hands on his trousers. "It's been years, Marek. No one's going to recognize me. I've changed. Besides, Finn and Makenna will be with me. No one's going to suspect a man traveling with those two rascals."

Marek's jaw tightened, and he shook his head. "Ellis' father is still the sheriff. His brothers are deputies. You might have changed, but the law hasn't. If they figure out who you are—"

"They won't," Gavin interrupted, his voice steady but firm. "And even if they did, I'll handle it. I'm not going to spend my life hiding like a scared dog."

Marek sighed, glancing toward the house where Finn and Makenna were emerging, chatting and laughing as they approached. "Just... be careful, all right? I don't want those two getting hurt."

Gavin's expression softened at the mention of the kids. "I'll be careful," he promised.

As they climbed into the wagon, Makenna took the reins with a confident grin. "Don't worry, Uncle Gavin. If anyone causes trouble, I'll charm them into forgetting their own name."

Gavin chuckled, though a flicker of unease remained in his chest. "Just focus on driving, darlin'."

The journey to town was pleasant, the siblings and Gavin sharing stories and laughter as the wagon rattled along the dusty road. But as they approached the outskirts of town, Gavin's eyes narrowed, scanning the familiar streets. He hadn't been here in nearly two decades, but some things never changed.

The sheriff's department sat prominently on the main road, its wooden sign swaying slightly in the breeze. Gavin's stomach tightened as they passed by, his gaze instinctively dropping to avoid attention.

"Hey, look who's coming over to talk to you," Finn said, nudging Makenna in a teasing manner.

A young man in a deputy's uniform was approaching, his hat tilted back to reveal a kind smile. He couldn't have been much older than Makenna, his sandy hair and freckled complexion giving him a boyish charm.

"Afternoon, Ms. Craite," he greeted, his eyes immediately drawn to Makenna. "I didn't know you were coming to town today."

Makenna raised an eyebrow, a teasing smile tugging at her lips. "That's because I'm an independent woman who goes where she wants as she wants, Henry."

"Well, Ms. Independence, it's still a very nice surprise." Henry said, adjusting his hat.

Henry's gaze flicked to Gavin, who sat stiffly in the back of the wagon. "And who might you be?"

"That's our uncle," Makenna said casually. "He's helping us out on the farm."

Gavin kept his expression neutral, tipping his hat slightly. "Afternoon."

Henry looked suspiciously at Gavin briefly, as if something about Gavin was not right. But the moment passed, and his focus returned to Makenna.

"Well, Miss, perhaps I'll call on you in the coming days?"

"Perhaps," she supplied.

"Well then, perhaps you'll let me escort you around town. I'd be happy to."

Finn rolled his eyes. "We're just here for cattle feed."

Makenna smirked at her brother before turning back to Henry. "My oh my Henry Grady, aren't you the gentleman. That sounds nice, but maybe another time. We're just making a quick trip today."

As Henry tipped his hat and stepped aside to let them continue, Gavin exhaled slowly, his hands gripping the edge of the wagon. Makenna gave him a curious look.

"Something wrong, Uncle Gavin?"

"No, darlin'," he said quietly. "Everything's fine."

But his mind raced as the wagon rolled on. Henry Grady. Ellis' youngest brother, perhaps? Now a man, and one who could unknowingly unravel everything.

Gavin clenched his jaw. He'd come too far to let the past catch up to him now.

Inside the sheriff's department, the air was lighthearted as Henry Grady walked in, whistling a cheerful tune. His two older brothers—Aaron and Nolan—looked up from their desks, smirks already forming on their faces.

"Well, well," Aaron drawled, leaning back in his chair. "Look who's back. Did you take the long way 'round town, Henry, or were you busy making eyes at some farmer's daughter?"

Henry rolled his eyes but couldn't hide the faint blush creeping up his neck. "I was just being polite."

"Polite," Nolan echoed with a laugh. "That what they're callin' it now? You've been gone near an hour, little brother. She must've been somethin' special."

"She is," Henry admitted, grabbing a cup of water from the cooler. "Name's Makenna Craite. Pretty as a picture, and sharp as a whip, too."

Nolan snorted. "Well, don't get too attached. If she's a Craite from around here, odds are she's trouble."

"Craite trouble," Aaron added, his tone teasing.

Before Henry could respond, the door to the back office swung open, and Sheriff Bill Grady strode out, his aged yet still imposing figure framed by the doorway. He was wiping his hands with a rag, his sharp eyes scanning the room. "What's this I'm hearing about trouble?"

"Nothing serious," Nolan said with a grin. "Henry's gone and found himself a girl. A Craite girl, no less."

Bill froze, his face darkening. "Craite?"

Henry hesitated, feeling the sudden shift in the room's atmosphere. "Yeah. Makenna Craite. They got that farm just outside of town."

Bill tossed the rag onto his desk and glared at Henry. "You stay away from that family, you hear me? They're no good. Always been trash, always will be."

"Aw, come on, Pa," Henry protested. "She seems nice, and—"

"I don't care how she seems!" Bill snapped, his voice cutting through the room. "You don't get involved with Craites. End of discussion."

The room fell silent for a moment, the tension thick. Then, trying to lighten the mood, Aaron leaned over and jabbed Henry in the ribs. "Guess you're out of luck, Romeo."

Henry scowled but stayed quiet, sensing it wasn't the time to push back. He drank his water in silence while Bill went back to organizing papers on his desk.

But as the mood started to settle, Henry remembered something. "She was with her uncle. Didn't even know she had one."

Bill's head snapped up so fast it was almost a blur. "Uncle?"

"Yeah," Henry said, looking at his father curiously. "Tall guy, dark hair, kind of rough-looking. Said he was helping them out on the farm. Don't think I caught his name, though."

Bill's face turned pale as he stormed past his desk toward the door.

Henry blinked, startled. "What's the big deal?"

"The big deal," Bill growled as he flung the door open, "is that family killed your brother!"

Henry's mouth dropped open; his water forgotten. "What?"

Nolan sighed, rubbing the back of his neck. "Ellis, Henry. You were just a kid, but yeah... it was the Craites. Marek's brother—what was his name?"

"Gavin," Nolan supplied grimly. "Gavin Craite."

Henry's head spun as he watched his father rush outside, his boots pounding against the wooden steps. Bill scanned the road, his eyes narrowing as he spotted the wagon in the distance, disappearing down the dusty trail.

"There's someone with them," Bill muttered, squinting against the sun. "But I can't see his face."

He turned sharply, pointing a finger at Henry. "You're gonna find out who that man is. Do you understand me?"

Henry's confusion deepened as he stammered, "I don't even know what's going on!"

Aaron sighed heavily, gesturing for Henry to sit down. "Look, Pa's been carrying this grudge for years. Ellis was murdered in cold blood by Gavin Craite. Then he ran off like a coward. We've been waiting for payback ever since."

Henry's jaw clenched as he absorbed this new information. The friendly smile of the girl he'd met that day flashed in his mind. "She doesn't seem like someone tied up in all that," he said softly.

"Doesn't matter," Nolan said firmly. "You're a Grady, and she's a Craite. That's all Pa's ever gonna see."

Outside, Bill paced the porch, his mind racing. If that man with the Craites was who he thought it was, this was far from over.

CHAPTER 25

A few days later, Henry rode up to the Craite farm, the late afternoon sun casting long shadows across the fields. He dismounted near the barn and tied his horse to the post, his heart beating just a little faster than normal. As he looked around, he spotted Makenna emerging from the barn with a bucket in hand. She paused when she saw him, then broke into a wide smile.

"Henry!" she called, setting the bucket down. "What brings you out here?"

"Thought I'd pay you a visit," he said, tipping his hat with a grin. "If that's alright with you."

"Of course it is," Makenna said, brushing her hands on her apron. "Come on, I'll show you around."

They spent the afternoon walking the property, the conversation easy and light. Makenna showed him the creek where she and Finn had played as children and the old apple tree where she liked to read. As the sun dipped lower, the sky turning shades of gold and pink, Makenna turned to him.

"Why don't you stay for dinner? I'm sure Ma and Pa won't mind."

Henry hesitated for a moment, knowing his family wouldn't approve, but he couldn't resist the chance to spend more time with her. "I'd like that," he said.

Inside the farmhouse, Shannon and Marek exchanged a quick glance when Makenna brought Henry into the kitchen.

"This is Henry," Makenna said brightly. "He rode out to visit, and I invited him to stay for dinner."

Marek offered a polite nod, his expression guarded. "Pleasure to meet you, Henry. I'm Marek, Makenna's father."

"And I'm Shannon," Shannon added, her smile warm but her eyes sharp as she studied him.

Gavin appeared in the doorway, his gaze instantly locking onto Henry. There was a flicker of recognition in his eyes, but he quickly masked it. "Evenin'," he said simply, his tone neutral.

"Evenin'," Henry replied, tipping his hat.

Dinner was served soon after, and the conversation started off pleasant enough. Marek asked Henry about his family, his work, and what had brought him to the Craite farm.

"Well," Henry began, setting his fork down, "I'm a deputy over in town. My pa's the sheriff."

The room seemed to freeze. Shannon's smile faltered, Marek's hand gripped his knife a little tighter, and Gavin's gaze sharpened.

"Oh?" Marek said, his tone carefully even. "Who's your pa?"

"Bill Grady," Henry said casually, oblivious to the tension that had suddenly filled the room.

Makenna blinked, confused by the sudden shift in mood. She glanced at Finn, who looked equally puzzled.

"Grady?" Marek repeated, his voice tightening.

Henry nodded, still smiling. "That's right. My brothers are Aaron and Nolan. I'm the youngest."

Gavin's jaw clenched, but he said nothing. Shannon quickly stepped in. "Well, isn't that something," she said, her voice overly bright. "Henry, would you like more potatoes?"

"No, thank you, ma'am," Henry said, leaning back in his chair. His eyes drifted to Gavin, who was staring at his plate. "So, Mr. Craite—what brings you to town?"

Gavin looked up; his expression guarded. "I'm just passin' through. Came to see my sister and help out a bit on the farm." He said trying to throw Henry off.

"Your sister?" Henry asked, raising an eyebrow. "I didn't know Makenna had an uncle."

"Just for a few weeks," Shannon interjected quickly. "He's always traveling."

Henry leaned back, his sharp eyes studying the

three adults. "Interesting," he said slowly. "You don't see many travelers settlin' down on a farm, though."

Marek forced a laugh, the sound brittle. "Gavin's an exception to the rule, I suppose."

Finn and Makenna exchanged another confused glance, but they stayed silent, sensing something was off.

Noticing the tension in the air, Henry decided to ease up. "Well, I reckon farm life must run in the family," he said lightly. "This is a fine place you've got here."

The room relaxed slightly, and the conversation shifted to less charged topics. But beneath the surface, the unease lingered. Henry couldn't shake the feeling that something about Gavin didn't add up, and the Craite's couldn't shake the fear that Henry might figure out who Gavin really was.

The sky had turned a dusky violet by the time Henry rose from the table, thanking Shannon for the meal. Marek walked him to the door, his expression as unreadable as ever, while Makenna trailed behind, a soft smile on her lips.

"Well, I best be heading back before it gets too dark," Henry said, adjusting his hat as he stepped onto the porch.

"Safe travels," Marek said, his voice gruff.

Henry turned to Makenna, his smile warming. "Thank you for letting me stay for dinner. I'll be back soon to see you again."

Makenna blushed, glancing at her father before stepping closer to Henry. "I'd like that," she said softly.

Henry hesitated for a moment, then leaned in, brushing a gentle kiss against her lips. It was chaste but filled with promise. Makenna's cheeks flushed as Henry stepped back, tipping his hat with a grin. "Goodnight, Miss Craite."

"Goodnight, Henry," she murmured, watching him mount his horse and ride off into the fading light.

Once his figure disappeared down the road, Marek turned to Makenna, his face grim. "Inside. Now."

The family gathered in the sitting room, the tension thick enough to cut with a knife. Finn and Makenna sat side by side, their expressions a mix of confusion and worry, while Shannon, Marek, and Gavin stood by the fireplace, exchanging uncertain glances.

Marek finally broke the silence, his voice firm. "You two deserve to know the truth. It's time."

Shannon took a deep breath, sitting down across from her children. "This isn't easy to talk about," she began, her voice trembling slightly. "But you need to understand what's at stake."

Gavin shifted uncomfortably; his hands clasped in front of him. "This goes back a long way," he said, his voice low. "To when your ma and I were about your age."

Shannon nodded; her eyes distant as she recalled the memories. "There was a man named Ellis Grady. He was trying to court me back then, but I wasn't interested. He didn't take rejection well."

Gavin's jaw tightened. "He became obsessed. He'd follow Shannon around, showing up wherever she was. One night, things went too far."

Shannon's voice wavered as she continued. "Ellis attacked us. He wanted to hurt Gavin, to scare him off so he could have me for himself. But he took it too far, he and his buddies beat Gavin nearly to death and then Ellis…took advantage of me."

"And I killed him for it." Gavin admitted, his tone heavy with regret.

Finn and Makenna's eyes widened in shock.

"He did it because of what Ellis had done to me." Shannon added quickly, her voice pleading. "Ellis was a monster. But Ellis' father, Bill, didn't see it that way."

"Bill's been after me ever since," Gavin said, his voice bitter. "He made it his life's mission to hunt me down. That's why I had to leave. Why you never knew the truth about me."

Finn leaned forward. "But we thought you were dead."

Shannon nodded. "We let everyone believe that, even you two. It was the only way to keep you safe."

"But now," Marek said, his voice grave, "with Henry coming around, things are getting dangerous. If Bill or his deputies find out Gavin's alive and here, they won't stop until they tear this family apart."

Makenna looked between her parents and Gavin, her face pale but resolute. "Henry doesn't even know about any of this. He's not like his father or brothers. He's... he's kind."

"Makenna," Shannon said gently, "he might be kind, but he's still a Grady. And if he finds out the truth..."

"He won't," Makenna interrupted, her voice firm. "I love him, and I'm not giving him up."

The room fell silent as everyone came to terms with her decision. Gavin finally spoke, his tone soft but serious. "Love's a powerful thing, lass. But it can also be dangerous. Especially with the Gradys involved."

Makenna squared her shoulders, her eyes blazing. "Then we'll just have to make sure Henry never finds out."

The family exchanged uneasy glances, the enormity of the situation sinking in. Shannon reached out to take Makenna's hand. "We'll protect you, no matter what. But you need to be careful. For all our sakes."

Makenna nodded; determination etched across her face. "I will be."

Gavin glanced out the window into the darkened yard, his jaw set. "We'll all have to be."

CHAPTER 26

The morning sun bathed the Craite farm in soft light, but the atmosphere inside the house was anything but calm. Shannon, Marek, and Gavin sat at the kitchen table, their voices low but urgent. Finn leaned against the doorframe, listening intently, while Makenna sat at the far end of the room, arms crossed, her expression set in quiet rebellion.

"We don't have many options," Marek said, his voice steady but heavy with resignation. "Bill's not going to stop until he finds you, Gavin. And if he figures out who you are…"

Gavin nodded; his jaw tight. "I can go back to Boston. It's a big enough city. I can disappear there again."

Shannon's hand shot out, gripping his arm. "You're not leaving me behind. Not again." Her voice was firm, but there was an undercurrent of desperation.

Gavin looked at her, his expression pained. "Shannon, I can't ask you to give up the life you've built here. Your family, the farm—this is your home."

"We are a family now," she said fiercely. "I've lived without you for too long, Gavin. I'm not doing it again."

Finn stepped forward, his voice breaking the tension. "If Ma's going, I'm going too."

Shannon turned to her son, her face softening. "Finn, you don't have to—"

"Yes, I do," he interrupted. "I've been wanting to leave Maple Creek anyway. Boston's a chance for me to get an education, to see the world. Besides, I'm not letting you go without me."

Marek shook his head, his expression unreadable. "I'm not leaving this farm. It's my responsibility, and I've put too much into it to walk away now." He glanced at Makenna. "And she's not going anywhere either."

Makenna straightened in her chair; her voice quiet but resolute. "I'm staying. I won't give up Henry or the life I've built here. I like it here and I'm not going to let everyone else's mistakes dictate my life."

A heavy silence fell over the room as the family absorbed the reality of their decisions. Finally, Shannon spoke, her voice trembling but determined. "Then it's settled. Gavin, Finn, and I will leave. Marek and Makenna will stay. If that's what you want, Makenna. We'll go to Boston and figure things out from there.

You'll always be welcome to come live with us."

Gavin looked down at his hands, his fingers curling into fists. "I hate this. Leaving like a coward. But if it's the only way to keep everyone safe…"

Marek nodded, standing. "We don't have much time. Start packing what you need."

The family worked quickly, gathering essentials and saying quiet goodbyes. Shannon packed a small trunk, her movements brisk and purposeful, while Finn helped Gavin sort through what little he had. Makenna lingered in the doorway, watching with a mixture of sadness and frustration.

The wagon was nearly packed, its bed loaded with trunks and supplies for the journey to Boston. Gavin tied the last bundle tightly, his hands steady despite the storm raging inside him. Their intentions would soon be interrupted by the distant clatter of horses' hooves and the low murmur of voices approaching. His gut told him exactly who it was.

Hearing the approaching riders, Marek moved to the window, his expression darkening.

"They're here," he said grimly.

From the corner of his eye, he saw Shannon standing at the kitchen window, her face pale and drawn. Marek moved to the front door, his stance rigid, while Finn lingered near his mother, gripping a rifle for protection. Makenna stood beside him, eyes wide with both fear and defiance.

Gavin adjusted the brim of his round hat, the

shadow falling over his eyes. He was in the back of the wagon sorting through trunks, searching. As the riders slowed down and moved into the yard, approaching the homestead, Gavin found what he had been searching for. Attaching his bandolier and holstering his pistol. A slow, steadying breath escaped him as he buckled the holster firmly around his waist. If trouble was coming, he wasn't about to hide from it.

From the porch, Bill Grady's voice carried across the yard like a thunderclap. "Morning, Marek. Heard Shannon's brother is in town. Thought I'd come by and make his acquaintance."

Marek didn't respond, his hands gripping the doorframe so tightly his knuckles turned white. Inside the house, Shannon whispered something to Finn, her voice trembling, but no one moved.

Gavin stepped around the side of the wagon, his boots crunching on the gravel. The wide brim of his hat hid his eyes, but the set of his jaw and the deliberate way he moved were unmistakable. He stopped a few paces from the porch, standing tall and calm, his hand resting lightly on the wagon's edge.

Bill turned, his cold, calculating eyes narrowing as they landed on him. The sheriff's sons in tow, stiffened behind him, their hands hovering near their own holsters.

Gavin emerged from behind the wagon, squinting in the sun and tilting his head slightly, his voice steady and sharp as steel. "You've been asking for me, Sheriff."

The air seemed to freeze, his words hanging heavy in the stillness.

Shannon stood at the doorway behind Marek, her face stricken, but her eyes locked on Gavin with a mixture of fear and pride. Marek shifted uncomfortably, his lips pressed into a tight line, while Finn and Makenna stood frozen inside.

Bill's lips curled into a slow, dangerous smile. "And that would make you…"

Gavin took a step forward, his hand brushing against the edge of his coat, just enough to reveal the pistol holstered at his hip. "Gavin Craite. I believe we've met once before and that you've been looking for me for quite some time."

The sheriff's sons exchanged glances, their postures tense. Bill's smile faltered for the briefest moment before his expression hardened.

"Well, well," Bill said, his voice low and venomous. "The balls on you, showing your face around here."

CHAPTER 27

Gavin shrugged; his gaze unwavering. "I guess time doesn't heal all wounds after all."

The tension in the yard was palpable, every eye fixed on the two men. For a moment, it seemed like the entire world had gone silent, waiting to see who would make the first move.

The yard felt like it was caught in a storm—silent but seething with tension. Gavin stood his ground, his hand resting on the wagon as Sheriff Grady stepped closer, his boots crunching the gravel with deliberate weight. The sheriff reached into his coat and pulled out a folded sheet of yellowed paper. He held it up, the edges fluttering in the breeze.

"No, I should say it does not. And besides, this isn't so much about me as it is about abiding by the law, which in these parts, is my business. A business I take quite seriously I might add." Bill's voice was calm, but it carried an edge sharp enough to cut through steel.

Gavin didn't flinch. His gaze dropped to the paper as Bill unfolded it with a snap. It was an old wanted poster, weathered and cracked from years of handling, but the name was unmistakable.

WANTED
GAVIN CRAITE
FOR THE
MURDER of ELLIS GRADY
$500 REWARD

The likeness was crude, but it was enough. Shannon's sharp intake of breath echoed from the porch. Finn's face went pale, and Makenna instinctively stepped closer to Henry, whose own expression was a mixture of confusion and regret.

"Well now, looks an awful lot like you, don't it?" Bill asked, his voice dangerously low.

Gavin's jaw tightened. "That was a long time ago."

Bill's eyes narrowed. "Not long enough." He stepped forward, the poster still in his hand. "Ellis was my son. My flesh and blood. You think I've forgotten?"

Gavin took a deep breath, his voice calm but firm. "Your son attacked Shannon. He didn't leave me much choice."

The sheriff's lips twisted into a sneer, his grief bubbling under the surface. "Choice? You call killing my boy a choice?"

"Defending her was my only choice," Gavin shot back, his voice rising slightly. "Ellis wasn't innocent. He preyed on women and was a god damned coward."

The words hung in the air like a challenge, and for a moment, the two men simply stared at each other, the weight of years pressing down on them.

Bill took another step forward, his voice cold. "I should shoot you where you stand. But fortunate for you, that's not the kind of man I am. If you surrender, right now, I'll take you in and you can stand trial for what you did."

Behind him, Nolan, Ellis' eldest brother, scoffed loudly. "Stand trial? Are you kidding me, Pa? He doesn't deserve a trial! He deserves a bullet for how he done Ellis!"

"Nolan, stay out of this," Bill snapped, his gaze never leaving Gavin.

Nolan stepped forward, his hand already on the butt of his pistol. "No, I won't. You think a trial's gonna bring Ellis back? You think it's justice? This bastard's been living free for twenty years while we buried our brother!"

Gavin's hand moved subtly to his side, hovering near his own weapon, but he didn't draw. His voice was steady as he said, "If you're looking for revenge, you won't find it here, Nolan. You'll end up joining your brother, I can assure you."

The words hit like a slap, and Nolan's face darkened with rage. He yanked his pistol free, pointing it at

Gavin. "Say that again. I dare you."

Bill spun; his voice thunderous. "Put that gun away, Nolan! You're not the law here—I am!"

The argument between father and son erupted, their voices loud and heated. Meanwhile, Henry, who had been standing silently, crossed the yard to Makenna. His expression was pained, his voice low and pleading.

"Makenna, I didn't know this was going to happen. I swear," he said, his eyes searching hers.

Makenna's face was pale, her hands trembling slightly as she looked at him. "You didn't know your father wanted to take my father, or uncle, or whatever he is, away? Or that your brother wanted to kill him?"

Henry shook his head. "I just… I just didn't know what was going to, it all happened so fast. I'm sorry Makenna, I didn't mean for this to happen."

She studied him for a long moment, her emotions warring between anger and the love she couldn't deny. "Henry, this… this, changes everything."

Before Henry could respond, a sharp voice cut through the chaos.

"Everyone quiet!" Shannon stepped off the porch, her voice trembling with emotion but commanding attention. She walked past Bill and Nolan, stopping beside Gavin.

"This ends here," she said firmly. "No more bloodshed. Bill, you want him to stand trial? Fine. Gavin, drop your belt and go with him. As rotten as Ellis is, Bill's always been a fair man. Marek will accompany you with them to town just to make sure."

Marek moved from the porch and stood behind Gavin.

Bill's eyes softened slightly, but his resolve didn't waver. "Listen to her Gavin. This is your last chance. Which by the way, is one more chance than you gave Ellis."

"Ellis had it coming," Shannon fired back, her voice rising. "You don't know what he did to me!"

The sheriff glared at Shannon, "Well, seeing as you're standing here defending this murderer, I'm guessing he didn't kill you."

The yard fell into a tense silence, everyone waiting to see what would happen next. Gavin's hand hovered near his pistol, Nolan's weapon was still raised, and Finn, who had inched his way into the fray, looked ready to jump in at a moment's notice.

Nolan, still pointing his gun at Gavin pleaded with his father. "C'mon Pa, let's just end it right here."

Bill spoke, his voice heavy. "Nolan, lower your gun. We're doing this my way."

The tension in the yard was razor-thin, ready to snap. Gavin's hand lingered near his holstered pistol, his stance calm but prepared. Across from him, Nolan's gun remained trained on him, unwavering, his knuckles white against the grip.

Bill Grady's voice was sharp and commanding. "Nolan, I said lower your damn gun!"

Nolan's jaw tightened, but he didn't move. Instead, Aaron, standing slightly behind his father, took a deliberate step forward, his face dark with fury.

"For once, I agree with Nolan," Aaron said, his tone cold. "An eye for an eye, Pa. He murdered Ellis, and now he's standing here like he's done nothing wrong. He doesn't deserve a trial. He deserves justice."

Bill spun on him, his voice rising. "You call this justice? Shooting a man down like a dog? That's not how we do things, Aaron!"

Aaron's face twisted with frustration. "Maybe it's not how you do things, but Ellis was our brother. I'm not standing by while this bastard walks away from what he did!"

The words struck like a hammer, and the charged atmosphere seemed to thicken. From the porch, Shannon stepped forward, her voice trembling but forceful. "Stop this! All of you! Bill, you're letting your hatred turn your sons into killers!"

Aaron ignored her, his hand dropping to his holster. "Enough talk. I'm ending this now."

It happened in an instant.

Aaron drew his pistol, the barrel rising in a blur of motion. But Gavin was faster—much faster.

With a fluidity that came from years of practice, his hand snapped to his side, fingers curling around the grip of his revolver. In one smooth motion, he pulled the gun from his holster and fired from the hip.

The crack of the shot shattered the air like a

thunderclap.

Aaron staggered backward, a red stain blooming across his chest as his pistol fell from his hand. His knees buckled, and he collapsed to the ground, clutching at the wound.

"No!" Nolan roared, his own gun snapping up as he fired, missing Gavin.

But Gavin was already turning, his second shot coming as naturally as breathing.

The bullet hit Nolan square in the shoulder, spinning him around with the force of the impact. His gun flew from his hand as he fell to the dirt, groaning in pain.

"Stop it!" Shannon screamed, running toward Gavin, her hands outstretched.

Gavin stood motionless, his pistol still raised, smoke curling from the barrel. His eyes were hard, his breathing steady, but there was no mistaking the turmoil beneath his calm exterior.

Gavin moved his pistol towards Bill, who had not yet drawn.

Bill was frozen, his face a mask of shock and fury. "You just shot my boys," he said, his voice low and deadly.

Gavin's voice was cold, though there was a tremor of regret in it. "They left me no choice."

Henry rushed to Aaron's side, pressing his hands against the wound in a desperate attempt to stem the bleeding. "Aaron, stay with me! Don't you dare die on me!"

Finn and Makenna stood frozen on the porch, their faces pale with fear and disbelief.

Shannon let out a scream. "Marek!"

Marek had fallen to the ground. The errant bullet from Nolan's pistol had struck him in the chest.

Bill finally moved, stepping toward Aaron, his hand trembling as it hovered near his holster. For a moment, it looked like he might draw, but Shannon stepped between them.

"Bill, stop," she said firmly, her voice breaking with emotion. "This has to end. Haven't we lost enough?"

Bill's eyes were wild, his breathing ragged. "He just shot my boys, Shannon. My boys."

"And they were about to shoot him and they shot Marek… who's the best out of the lot of you." Shannon replied, tears streaming down her face. "If you kill Gavin now, what will it solve? More bloodshed? More grief?"

Bill's shoulders sagged, the honesty of what she was pressing down on him. He looked at Aaron, writhing in the dirt, then at Nolan, groaning and clutching his shoulder. Slowly, his hand fell away from his holster.

The yard was in chaos as Henry tended to Nolan, Finn and Makenna holding Marek's body who was quickly fading and Aaron laying lifeless next to the wagon. Bill stood frozen in place, his fury simmering just beneath the surface. His eyes burned as he watched Gavin, who stood tall, his hand still lingering near his holster.

Then, in a blur of motion, Bill grabbed Shannon.

Her startled cry pierced the air as Bill pulled her against him, his pistol pressed to her temple. "It's over now!" he bellowed, his voice raw with rage. "Nobody moves, or she dies!"

Makenna screamed from where she knelt beside Marek, who had taken his last breath, blood pooling beneath him. Finn pressed his hands against the wound, his face pale. "Stay with us, Dad," he said with a futile plea and his voice shaking.

"Bill, don't do this!" Shannon cried, tears streaming down her face.

Henry froze, his hands raised. "Pa, let her go! You don't have to do this!"

Bill's face twisted with grief and rage as he glared at his youngest son. "You! Get to town and bring the marshal! Now!"

Henry hesitated, torn between obeying his father and standing his ground. He looked to Makenna, her face stricken with disbelief in what had just occurred, then to Shannon, who shook her head, silently begging him to stay.

"Go, Henry!" Bill barked, his voice cracking. "Do as I say, for once in your god damned life!"

Reluctantly, Henry mounted his horse. He cast one last desperate glance at Makenna, then spurred his horse and rode off toward town.

The dust from Henry's horse settled as silence fell

over the yard. Bill tightened his grip on Shannon, dragging her forward a few steps. His gun never wavered. "You've done it now, Craite," he spat, his voice venomous. "There'll be no trial after this. I'm gonna put you down right here, for what you've done."

Gavin took a step forward, his hands raised, his face calm but determined. "Bill, listen to me. You've been chasing a lie for twenty years. You think I killed Ellis in cold blood, but you don't know the truth."

Bill sneered, his grip on Shannon unrelenting. "The truth? The truth is you murdered my son and ran like a coward. You think I'll believe a word out of your mouth now?"

Gavin's voice hardened. "Ellis raped Shannon."

The words hung in the air, a deafening silence following their impact.

Bill's face contorted with disbelief. "You lying son of a—"

"It's true!" Shannon shouted, cutting him off. Her voice was raw and trembling, but she stood firm, even with Bill's pistol pressed to her head. "Ellis attacked me. He was jealous and angry because I wouldn't be with him. He didn't care what I wanted. He—" Her voice broke, and she sobbed. "He hurt me, Bill. And when Gavin found out, he was overcome with rage. He wasn't thinking straight. What would you have done?"

Bill's hand shook, the pistol quivering against Shannon's temple. His eyes darted between her and

Gavin, searching for any sign of deceit. "You're lying," he said hoarsely. "You're trying to save him."

"I'm not," Shannon said, her voice soft but unwavering. "I swear on everything I hold dear, it's the truth."

Bill's breath came in ragged gasps, his mind reeling. His grip on Shannon loosened slightly, but the gun remained in place. "No," he whispered. "Not my boy. Ellis wouldn't have done that."

Gavin took another cautious step forward. "I didn't want to kill him, Bill. But when I found out what he'd done, I couldn't let it stand. You would've done the same if it had been your wife or daughter."

Bill's eyes filled with tears, his face a mix of anguish and fury. "You had no right to take him from me!"

Gavin's voice dropped, steady and low. "He left me no choice. Just like you're leaving me none now."

From the porch, Finn and Makenna watched helplessly. Finn's hands were still pressed against Marek's lifeless body.

Makenna looked to her mother, then to Gavin. "Ma, do something!" she begged.

The chaos in the yard quieted, but its echoes still hung heavy in the air. The sun dipped lower, casting long, jagged shadows as if the earth itself was trying to hide the bloodshed. Bill stood in the middle of it all, his chest heaving as he looked down at his hands, one still gripping Shannon, the other holding the pistol.

His eldest son Nolan lay slumped against the

wagon, coughing weakly as his lifeblood spilled out. He mustered the strength to speak. "… it's true Pa…I was there… it's true what they're saying about …Ellis. We didn't know he was gonna do that."

Nolan's revelation crushed Bill, and his grip on Shannon loosened.

"What have I done?" he muttered, his voice barely audible.

Shannon stumbled back, tears streaming down her face as she clutched her arms to her chest. Finn and Makenna, still kneeling by Marek, froze, watching Bill as he staggered a step forward. His gun hung limply at his side now, the fight gone out of him.

"What have I done?" he repeated, louder this time, his eyes wide and unfocused. His gaze darted around the yard—at Nolan, Aaron, Marek, and finally to Gavin.

Gavin stood still, his pistol back in its holster, his expression unreadable. "Bill…" he began cautiously, but the sheriff barely seemed to hear him.

"I was just… I was trying to make it right," Bill muttered, his voice cracking. He dropped the pistol from his side, the weapon landing in the dirt with a soft thud. His knees buckled slightly, but he caught himself, running a trembling hand over his face.

His eyes flicked to Aaron again, and the sight seemed to shatter him. He dropped to his knees in the dirt, gripping his head with both hands. "I didn't want this… I didn't mean for this…"

"Pa," Nolan rasped weakly from where he was leaning, but Bill didn't move to him.

Instead, he reached for the fallen pistol, his fingers curling around the grip. He stood shakily, his face pale and his eyes distant.

"Bill, no!" Shannon cried, stepping forward, but Gavin caught her arm and pulled her back.

"What have I done?" Bill whispered one final time, his voice hollow and distant. His shoulders sagged under the unbearable weight of his actions. His hand trembled as he raised the pistol, pressing the cold barrel to his temple.

"No!" Makenna screamed, scrambling to her feet, but it was too late.

The gunshot cracked through the still air, startling the horses and sending a flock of crows scattering from the trees. Bill crumpled to the ground, lifeless.

For a moment, no one moved. The yard was eerily silent, save for the soft groan of Nolan and the faint rustle of leaves in the breeze.

Makenna fell to her knees, sobbing into her hands. Finn sat frozen beside Marek, his face pale and his eyes wide. Shannon stared at Bill's body, her hands covering her mouth as tears streamed down her face.

Gavin stepped forward, his boots crunching on the dirt. He stopped beside Bill's body, his face grim but stoic. For a long moment, he simply stared down at the man who had been his enemy for so long, his expression unreadable.

Shannon's voice broke the silence, raw and trembling. "What are we going to do now?"

Gavin glanced at her, then at the devastation around them—the broken family, the spilled blood, the loss that could never be undone. His voice was quiet but resolute as he finally answered, "I don't know, Shannon."

The shadows grew longer as the sun set on the shattered lives in the yard, and the truth of what had transpired settled heavily on them all.

CHAPTER 28

Henry rode into town yelling for Marshal Wheeler and word quickly spread about the violent confrontation at the Craite farm. The local marshal, a man named William Wheeler, was in the street speaking with a local when Henry found him and told him what had occurred.

Marshal William Wheeler, a stout man with a weathered face and a calm demeanor, raised a hand to steady Henry's frantic words. His pale blue eyes narrowed beneath the brim of his hat as he listened. Around them, curious townsfolk began to gather, murmuring among themselves.

"Slow down, son," Wheeler said firmly, his voice carrying the authority of a man used to handling crises. "Tell me what happened."

Henry, still astride his horse, leaned down, gripping the saddle horn as he spoke, his words tumbling out in a rush. "There's been a shootout at the Craite farm. Pa's there with Nolan and Aaron, and—" his voice faltered, a flicker of grief breaking through his panic, "Aaron's dead, Marshal. Nolan's been shot, too, and Pa… Pa's lost his mind."

Wheeler's expression darkened, his jaw tightening. "Who did the shooting?"

"It's Gavin Craite," Henry said, his voice cracking. "He's alive, Marshal. After all these years. He… he killed Aaron, shot Nolan. Pa's threatening people. He told me to come ride for you."

The marshal turned to his deputy, a wiry young man named Jed, who had just stepped out of the general store with a coffee in hand. "Jed, saddle up. We're heading out."

"Yes, sir," Jed replied, already moving toward the livery stable.

Wheeler looked back at Henry; his expression steady but grave. "You've done the right thing coming to get me. Now, is anyone else hurt?"

Henry hesitated, rubbing the back of his neck as he recalled the scene. "Marek Craite was hit. Looked bad, I can't say that he was still breathing when I left. Finn and Makenna—Marek's kids—were trying to help him. Shannon… she's there, too. She and Pa are." He caught himself. "I don't know what's going on, we need to get out there straight away." Shame creeping into his voice. "Pa was holding her, using her to get to Gavin. He's not thinking straight, Marshal. I don't know what he's going to do."

Wheeler let out a heavy sigh, pulling his gun belt tighter. "Alright. We'll ride out there and put an end to this."

"Marshal," Henry said quickly, his face pale, "you've got to understand—this isn't just about Pa wanting justice. He's been after Gavin for years, since Ellis—"

"I know the history," Wheeler interrupted, his voice low and firm. "I've heard it all before. But whatever this is, it's gone too far." He paused, his expression softening slightly as he looked at the young man. "You did the right thing, Henry. Stay here in town. We'll take it from here."

Henry shook his head fiercely. "No. I'm coming with you. Pa's my responsibility, and I need to make this right."

Wheeler studied Henry for a long moment, then gave a curt nod. "Fine. But you stay out of the way and let me handle it. Is that clear?"

"Yes, sir," Henry said, straightening in his saddle.

As Wheeler and Henry prepared to leave, townsfolk whispered among themselves, speculating about the confrontation at the farm. Jed returned with their horses, leading the marshal's sturdy bay gelding.

Wheeler mounted up, adjusting his hat as he addressed the gathered crowd. "Go back to your business. This isn't a spectacle."

The crowd reluctantly dispersed, though many eyes lingered on the marshal and his companions as they rode out of town toward the Craite farm, the tension thick in the air.

The sun climbed higher in the sky, casting harsh light on the trail ahead. Wheeler's mind raced with thoughts of how to diffuse the situation, but deep down, he knew this confrontation had been a long time coming. It was bound to end one way or another—peacefully or in bloodshed.

The ride to the Craite farm was heavy with tension. Marshal Wheeler rode at the head of the group, his expression grim and unreadable. Beside him, Deputies Jed McFarlane and Roy Connelly kept pace, their usually easygoing demeanors replaced by quiet vigilance. Henry trailed slightly behind, his thoughts racing as the weight of what had transpired pressed down on him like a lead blanket.

The morning sun had burned away the cool air, leaving the trail dusty and dry. The faint smell of smoke carried on the wind, drawing a frown from Wheeler. He glanced back at Henry.

"Fire?" Wheeler asked.

Henry shook his head. "Not when I left. Could be the stove at the farm."

Wheeler nodded, but his instincts told him otherwise. The Craite farm was a place where tension had festered for years, and now it had erupted.

As they crested a low hill, the farm came into view. The scene before them was both eerily quiet and devastating. A plume of smoke rose lazily from the smoldering remains of a small shed near the barn. The main house stood intact, but its door hung open, swinging gently in the breeze.

The scene before them was grim and raw—a tableau of violence and heartbreak.

Aaron's lifeless body lay sprawled near the porch steps, a pool of blood darkening the earth around him. Marek was slumped against Finn, unmoving. Finn's hands stained with blood; his face stricken with grief. Nearby, Shannon and Makenna hovered over Nolan, who was pale and gasping for breath, his shirt soaked with crimson.

Marshal Wheeler dismounted slowly, his face a mask of controlled composure. He scanned the scene, taking in every detail. His deputies followed suit, their hands resting on their holstered pistols.

"Sweet mercy," Jed muttered, his voice low.

Shannon looked up; her face streaked with tears. "Marshal, he's still alive," she said, gesturing to Nolan. "He needs a doctor."

Wheeler nodded sharply. "Roy, take him to Doc Maynard. Now."

Roy hesitated, glancing at Wheeler for confirmation.

"Go!" Wheeler barked, and Roy sprang into action, carefully lifting Nolan and carrying him to his horse.

As Roy rode off, Wheeler turned his gaze to the others. His eyes landed on Gavin, who stood near Marek, his hat clutched in one hand, his face a stoic mask.

"Gavin Craite," Wheeler said, his voice steady but firm. "You've got some explaining to do."

Finn rose to his feet, stepping protectively in front of him. "He didn't start this, Marshal," Finn said, his voice trembling with emotion. "Bill and his sons came here looking for blood. They brought this on themselves!"

Wheeler held up a hand to silence him. "Stand down, boy. This isn't your fight."

"It's my family!" Finn shot back; his fists clenched.

Gavin placed a firm hand on Finn's shoulder, his voice calm but commanding. "Finn, that's enough."

Finn turned to him, his eyes pleading. "You can't just—"

"This has been a long time coming," Gavin said quietly, his gaze steady. "I don't wanna run no more."

Finn's shoulders sagged, and he stepped back reluctantly, his jaw clenched.

Wheeler nodded, stepping closer. "Gavin Craite, I'm placing you under arrest for the murder of Ellis Grady and for your involvement in the deaths here today."

Gavin complied with the Marshal's orders.

Shannon ran up to Gavin. "I can't lose you again." She protested.

"I'm no god damned good Shannon. You deserve so much more than this."

Shannon tried holding onto Gavin, but the

marshal and his deputy pulled him away.

Jed stepped forward, pulling out a length of rope to bind Gavin's hands. As he did, Wheeler looked to the remaining deputies. "Jed, start investigating this scene. I want to know exactly what happened and who fired the first shot."

"Yes, sir," Jed replied, handing the reins of the rope binding Gavin's hands over to the marshal then moving toward Aaron's body to begin his work.

Wheeler turned back to Shannon, his expression softening. "Miss Shannon, I'm sorry for what's happened here. We'll get it all sorted out, but for now, I need your cooperation."

Shannon nodded, though her face was pale and strained.

As Wheeler and his men prepared to leave, Gavin glanced back at Finn. "Take care of our family, boy. That's your job now."

Finn swallowed hard, his fists still trembling at his sides. "I will. I swear it. I wish I had gotten to know you better."

With that, the Marshal and his posse rode off, leaving what was left of the Craite family to pick up the shattered pieces of their lives.

CHAPTER 29

Later that evening, Father O'Connell waited patiently outside the dimly lit cell that Gavin occupied, the sounds of the bustling town outside muffled by the heavy wooden door. Gavin felt a pang of regret but also a sense of peace in knowing he had protected Finn. With the paper and a pencil the priest had given him, he began to write.

To My Family,

As I sit here in this cold, quiet cell awaiting the outcome of my fate, I find my thoughts consumed by you—my family. I write this letter with a heavy heart but a clear conscience. My choices, right or wrong, have led us all to this place. I do not seek your forgiveness, for I know my actions cannot be undone, but I do hope you understand the reasons behind them.

From the moment Ellis Grady wronged us, I made

decisions to protect those I love. I took a path that no man should ever have to walk, and though I regret the pain it has caused, I would do it again if it meant keeping you safe. My hope now is that you can build a better life, free from the shadows of my mistakes.

I leave you this letter not as a burden, but as a guide. In Boston, at the Provident Institution for Savings on Tremont Street, you will find the means to secure a future. I hold an account there under the number 747856. I have left explicit instructions with the bank that upon my passing, the entirety of the funds is to be released to Marek Craite or, in his absence, his widow.

To access the funds, you must provide this letter as well as identification to confirm your identity as my family. I have entrusted Father O'Connell to witness this letter, ensuring its validity and my intentions. Speak with him should you need assistance navigating this matter.

Though I am not there to guide you in person, I leave you with this advice: cherish each other. Life is fleeting and precious, and the bond of family is the greatest strength you will ever have. Protect it, nurture it, and never take it for granted.

Finn, you are a strong and intelligent young man. Be the pillar your family can lean on. Makenna, your spirit is bright and unyielding; let it light the way for those around you. Shannon, my love, your courage and love have held this family together. Do not let my mistakes overshadow the good you can still do.

I ask only that you remember me as a man who loved

you all fiercely, even when my actions betrayed that love.
May God watch over you always.
Yours in heart and spirit,

Gavin Craite

Witnessed by:

Father Michael O'Connell
St. Brigid's Church, Maple Creek – June 18, 1876.

With each word he wrote, he poured his heart into the letter, hoping that one day Finn, Makenna and Shannon would understand the choices he had made. As he signed his name, a heavy sense of resolve settled over him.

"You get this letter in the hands of Shannon Craite. No one else. You swear it." Gavin insisted grabbing onto the Father O'Connell's garment.

"May the Lord strike me down should I be untrue to my word. I will get this letter into the hands of Shannon Craite. And may God have mercy on your soul," proclaimed Father O'Connell.

With those words the good father was off. Gavin sat back down, hung his head and prayed for his brother.

CHAPTER 30

Months had gone by as Gavin awaited his trial with no word from Shannon, Makenna or Finn and no news of their whereabouts. On the day of his trial, the iron door to Gavin's cell creaked open, breaking the silence of the dim, musty room. He looked up from the small wooden bench, expecting the usual deputy, but instead, a well-dressed man with a sharp look in his eyes and a leather satchel in his hand stepped in.

"Mr. Craite," the man said, tipping his hat slightly. "My name is Elijah Hollister. I'm an attorney based out of Helena, and I've been retained to represent you at your trial."

Gavin blinked, caught off guard. "I wasn't aware I had the means for a lawyer, let alone someone of your stature."

Elijah offered a faint smile, setting his satchel down

on the rickety table. "Your family sent for me. They've ensured that I have everything I need to handle your case properly."

"My family?" Gavin's voice was hoarse, thick with disbelief. He leaned forward, resting his forearms on his knees. "I haven't seen them since I was brought here. How…how are they?"

"They're well," Elijah replied, his voice even. "And determined to see you through this. But let's not waste time—there are a few things we need to discuss before we step into that courtroom."

Gavin sat up straighter, his instincts sharpening. "Let me save you some time. I killed those men, Mr. Hollister. That much isn't up for debate."

Elijah pulled out a stack of papers and set them down with purpose. "You're not wrong, but the law isn't always black and white. Circumstances matter, Mr. Craite. What we'll argue is whether the killings were acts of self-defence, born out of desperation to protect your family. And, whether the Grady family's long-standing feud with yours contributed to the events that unfolded."

Gavin shook his head. "That judge won't care about circumstances. I've got blood on my hands, and that's all he'll see."

Elijah leaned forward; his eyes intense. "Judge Morgan Blake is many things, but he's not blind to the truth. And I've never walked into a courtroom without believing there's a chance to win. You owe it to your family to let me fight for you."

Gavin studied the man for a long moment, then nodded slowly. "Alright, Mr. Hollister. Let's get on with it."

The courtroom was abuzz with murmurs as Gavin was led in, shackles clinking with each step. The gallery was filled to capacity—townsfolk who had come to witness the trial of the year.

But as Gavin's eyes scanned the room, his breath caught in his throat. Sitting near the front, dressed in their very best, were Shannon, Finn, and Makenna. Shannon's dress was a deep emerald green, her face serene yet determined. Finn, now looking more like a young man than a boy, wore a crisp suit, his posture straight and proud. Makenna, radiant and poised, met his gaze with a small, reassuring smile.

They looked healthy, strong—different from the last time he'd seen them. A wave of emotion crashed over Gavin, but he swallowed it down, forcing himself to focus as Elijah placed a hand on his shoulder.

"Keep your head up, Mr. Craite," Elijah murmured. "You're not alone in this fight."

Judge Blake entered the courtroom, his gavel echoing as the room fell silent. The trial was about to begin.

The gavel struck hard, silencing the murmurs in the packed courtroom. Judge Morgan Blake adjusted his spectacles and leaned forward, his gaze piercing. "This court is now in session for the trial of Gavin

Craite, charged with multiple counts of murder. Let the proceedings begin."

Gavin sat at the defendant's table, flanked by Elijah Hollister. The seasoned attorney whispered a final reminder to remain composed as the prosecution launched into their opening statement.

The prosecutor, a wiry man with a sharp tone named Harold Fitch, began. "Ladies and gentlemen of the jury, what we have here is not a case of self-defence but cold-blooded murder. The accused, Mr. Craite, has a history of violence, and on that fateful day, he ended the life of Deputy Aaron Grady who was acting in the course of his duties as an officer of the law, by attempting to take Mr. Craite into custody for the murder of one Ellis Grady, many years prior. Mr. Craite then opened fire on Aaron and his brother Nolan—leaving Deputy Nolan Grady with a bullet in his shoulder and their father, Sheriff Bill Grady, to take his own life in despair."

Fitch paced, his voice rising. "The evidence will show that Mr. Craite is no innocent man. He's a fugitive with a record stretching back twenty years. This trial is not just about justice for the Grady family but ensuring that a man who has evaded the law for too long finally pays for his crimes."

Elijah stood next, his voice steady and calm. "Members of the jury, this case is not as simple as the prosecution would have you believe. The events of that day were born out of decades of unresolved conflict and the Grady family's decision to seek vengeance—not justice. Mr. Craite acted to protect his family against men who came to his home armed and intent on bloodshed. We will prove that the accused was left with no choice but to defend his loved ones."

The testimony began. Shannon was called to the stand, her face pale but resolute as she swore to tell the truth.

"Mrs. Craite," Elijah began, his tone soft but clear, "please tell the court what happened on the day in question."

Shannon gripped the edges of the stand, her voice trembling but growing stronger with each word. "It started early that morning. Gavin was preparing to leave the farm…to spare us from trouble. But then Bill Grady and his sons arrived, armed and angry. They accused Gavin of murder, demanded vengeance for the death of Ellis Grady—"

"Ellis Grady," Elijah interrupted gently, "can you tell the court about your history with him?"

Shannon closed her eyes briefly, then opened them, her gaze direct. "Ellis Grady was a monster. He attacked me, years ago, when I was a young woman. He assaulted me sexually and threatened to kill me if I told anyone. Gavin, whom I was in a relationship with, found out and…he did what he thought was right. He protected me."

The courtroom erupted into murmurs, the judge's gavel striking the bench to restore order.

"Continue, Mrs. Craite," Elijah urged.

"When Bill and his sons came to our farm," Shannon said, her voice cracking, "they didn't come for justice. They came for revenge. Aaron and Nolan drew their guns. Gavin—he only fired to protect us. To protect his family."

The prosecution's cross-examination was fierce, but Shannon held firm, her testimony unwavering.

Then it was Gavin's turn.

He stood tall, his chains clinking softly as he made his way to the stand. The courtroom fell silent, all eyes on the man who had been the center of so much turmoil.

Elijah approached him. "Mr. Craite, you've heard the testimony. You've seen the charges laid against you. Why don't you tell the court, in your own words, what happened that day?"

Gavin looked at the jury, his voice calm but laced with emotion. "I've made mistakes in my life, plenty of them. But that day, I didn't wake up wanting to kill anyone. Bill Grady and his sons came to my farm with guns and hate in their hearts. They threatened my family. I defended them. I'd do it again if it meant keeping them safe."

Finally, Henry was called to the stand. The room was tense as he approached, his boots heavy on the wooden floor. He sat down, avoiding eye contact with everyone but the judge.

"Mr. Grady," Elijah said carefully, "you were there

that day. You saw what happened. Can you tell the court what your father and brothers intended when they rode to the Craite farm?"

Henry hesitated, his hands clenching the edge of the stand. "They wanted blood," he finally said, his voice barely above a whisper. "My father was a good man. We all know this. But, he…he was so broken after Ellis. He did try to arrest Gavin peacefully, but Aaron took it too far and couldn't see reason. He convinced himself that Mr. Craite was a monster who had to pay."

The prosecutor objected, but the judge allowed Henry to continue.

"Myself and my father went there in the name of the law, but Nolan and Aaron…they didn't go there for justice," Henry said, his voice growing steadier. "They went to kill him. I didn't realize it until it was too late. My brothers drew first. They were ready to shoot. Mr. Craite didn't have a choice."

The significance of Henry's testimony hung heavy in the room. For the first time, the jury saw the truth in the chaos: a family driven to violence by their own grief, and a man who had done whatever he could to protect those he loved.

The gavel struck sharply, silencing the courtroom. Judge Morgan Blake removed his spectacles and leaned forward, his eyes scanning the room with a heavy expression. He rested his hands on the bench and exhaled deeply, the hardship of the case clearly bearing down on him.

"This has been one of the most difficult cases I've presided over," Judge Blake began, his voice resonating with authority and sorrow. "It is not often that a man stands before this court whose actions cannot be cleanly divided into right or wrong, guilty or innocent. But such is the nature of this trial."

The room was silent, save for the creak of wooden benches as people leaned in to hear every word.

"Gavin Craite," the judge said, fixing his gaze on the defendant, "there is no doubt that you are a man with a complicated past. The evidence presented, along with your own testimony, has painted a picture of a man shaped by hardship, who has made choices—both good and bad—in the name of protecting his loved ones."

Gavin held the judge's gaze, his face impassive, though his hands gripped the edge of the table tightly.

"The testimony we have heard from Mrs. Shannon Craite and others makes it clear that the events at the farm were not instigated by you, but by a family consumed with grief and revenge. And yet..." The judge's voice grew firmer. "The law is the law. While I am sympathetic to your circumstances, the fact remains that you are the lone suspect and solely accused of a murder from some 20 years ago, as well as another involving an officer of the law, not to mention the Grady's father took his own life as a direct consequence of the violence that unfolded that day."

Shannon's face crumpled, but she held herself upright, her hands trembling in her lap. Makenna gripped her mother's arm for support.

Judge Blake continued. "However, regarding the murder of Ellis Grady, the prosecution has failed to produce a single witness to provide testimony and prove beyond reasonable doubt that your actions constituted premeditated murder or that you had committed murder at all. Therefore, I cannot, according to our laws, find you guilty of his murder. In the case of Aaron Grady's murder and the subsequent shooting of his brother Nolan, both of whom were deputies in this territory at the time of the incident: the evidence shows that you acted in defense of your family, and for that, this court cannot condemn you as a murderer. That being said..." He paused, his voice dropping to a somber tone. "You did fire and strike deputy Nolan Grady who was acting within the course of his duties as a lawman, Mr. Craite, and for that, there must be accountability."

A murmur rippled through the courtroom, quickly silenced by the gavel.

"I hereby find Gavin Craite guilty of attempted manslaughter of an officer of the law," the judge declared. "For this crime, I sentence you to ten years in prison."

Gasps filled the room, followed by the low hum of hushed conversations. Gavin closed his eyes, his head bowing slightly. Relief and anguish warred within him. He had avoided the gallows, but the thought of ten more years away from his family felt like a life sentence in itself.

As the courtroom emptied, Shannon and Makenna approached him. A deputy stood nearby, but the man mercifully gave them a moment.

"Gavin," Shannon whispered, her voice thick with emotion. Tears glistened in her eyes, but her chin was raised defiantly. "I'll wait for you. No matter how long it takes. I'll wait."

Gavin met her gaze, his own eyes heavy with unspoken words. He reached for her hand through the bars of the holding area and clasped it tightly. "Don't waste your life waiting on me, Shannon. You and the kids deserve more than this."

Her lips trembled, but her voice was steady. "We're your family, Gavin. There's no more without you. When you're out, you'll come to Boston. That's where we'll be. We'll start fresh."

Makenna stepped forward, her chin quivering. "We'll be there, Pa. No matter what."

Gavin's throat tightened as he nodded, his grip on Shannon's hand never wavering. "I'll find you. I swear it."

The marshal approached then, his expression apologetic but firm. "Time's up."

Shannon leaned forward, pressing a kiss to Gavin's knuckles. "Stay strong. We'll be waiting."

As Gavin was led away, the weight of the sentence

hung heavy, but so did the glimmer of hope. The bonds of his family were unbroken, even as the world around them sought to tear them apart.

CHAPTER 31

The seasons rolled by like pages turning in a book, each one carrying its own weight of time and distance. In Boston, the air shifted with the rhythm of the year. The snow of winter blanketed the streets in silence, muffling the world outside Shannon's kitchen window. She would often sit there in the early mornings, a steaming cup of tea in her hands, her eyes gazing out as if willing the horizon to deliver Gavin back to her.

Letters traveled between Boston and the prison, carrying words that bridged the chasm of time. Shannon wrote to Gavin faithfully, pouring her thoughts and feelings onto the paper. She shared news of Finn and Makenna, now grown into thoughtful and productive adults. Makenna's sharp wit and love of books mirrored Gavin's own quiet intelligence, while Finn's strong, steady demeanor reminded Shannon of the man she had once fallen in love with so deeply. Gavin's responses were sparse but heartfelt, filled with promises of a future together and questions about the life he longed to rejoin.

Spring came with the sound of rain tapping against the windows and the scent of earth awakening after the frost. Shannon tended to the small garden behind the house, coaxing life from the soil as she coaxed hope into her heart. She imagined Gavin walking through the rows of flowers and vegetables, his hands brushing the leaves, his voice filling the air again. Each new sprout felt like a whisper of promise, a reminder that life, no matter how distant, would renew itself.

Summer brought golden sunlight that warmed the city streets and painted the harbor's waters with sparkling reflections. Finn and Makenna busied themselves with their own pursuits and relationships—Makenna having found a love of her own had settled down and started a family. Finn took on work at a local carpentry shop and had also found a woman to love and bring new life into their family. They spoke of their father often, their voices filled with a mix of longing and quiet admiration. Shannon's heart ached as she watched their family grow, knowing Gavin missed these moments but hopeful for the day they could all be together again.

Autumn arrived with the rustle of falling leaves and the scent of wood smoke drifting through the air. Shannon would sit by the fire in the evenings, rereading Gavin's letters, her fingers tracing the faded ink. She found comfort in the steady rhythm of his words, even as the nights grew longer and colder.

In the quiet of winter's return, the world seemed to pause, holding its breath. The years had been long, but Shannon's love for Gavin never wavered.

***

Ten years had passed. It was a drizzling morning, the rain casting a sombre but calm and quiet mood across the sprawling countryside. The air was still, save for the gentle rustling of the trees lining the gravel lane that stretched toward a pristine white colonial-style home. The house stood proud and serene, its wide porch adorned with rocking chairs and flower boxes bursting with color.

A figure appeared at the end of the lane; his silhouette framed by the morning light trying to break through the clouds. He walked slowly, each step purposeful, a small bag slung over his shoulder. His boots crunched softly against the gravel as he approached, his posture straight but marked by the passage of time.

Inside the house, Shannon stood at the window. Her hands were busy wiping the last of the morning dishes, her gaze was drawn to the figure moving up the lane. Her breath caught as she saw the figure nearing, and the plate slipped from her fingers into the soapy water.

Without hesitation, she threw open the door and ran down the porch steps, her heart pounding in her chest. She slowed only briefly, as if doubting her own eyes, before quickening her pace again.

The man stopped in his tracks, lowering his bag to the ground as she reached him. They stood there, face to face, both visibly older but still undeniably themselves. The lines on their faces told stories of years passed, of struggles and hopes carried in silence.

Her voice broke as she whispered, "Gavin."

He didn't speak. He opened his arms, and she fell into them, her sobs muffled against his chest. He held her tightly, his hand trembling as it cradled the back of her head. Tears slipped silently down his weathered face, disappearing into her hair.

They stayed that way, locked in an embrace that spoke more than words ever could. The world around them seemed to fade, leaving only the two of them in a moment suspended by time.

Finally, she pulled back just enough to look at him, her hands cupping his face. "You made it," she said, her voice shaking but filled with relief.

"I told you I would find you," he replied, his voice hoarse and thick with emotion.

They embraced again, tighter this time, as if to make up for all the years lost. As the sun broke through the clouds, casting the world in a soft amber glow, their tears mingled with laughter, and the promise of a new chapter began.

The house stood as witness; its porch bathed in the warm light of homecoming.

The End.

ACKNOWLEDGMENTS

I'd like to thank Fay Thompson and Big Moose Publishing for their continued support and dedication in helping me make this dream come true.

ABOUT THE AUTHOR

Patrick C Duffy is a happy husband and a proud father, who has lived all over Canada and travelled most of the world while serving with the Canadian Forces and now calls Saskatoon home.

This is his second book.